A Candlelight Ecstasy Romance™

SHE FELT THE POUNDING THUNDER OF HIS HEART

Karyn felt his body shudder and he groaned her name before gathering her ever closer to him. His hands moved restlessly over her, his trailing fingers faithfully following the line of her body from her smooth shoulders down across the side of her breast, the inward curve of her waist, the swell of her hips to her silky thighs. She was urgently aware of him. She sensed his desperate need and trembled, moved by the raw desire she saw reflected in the molten depths of his eyes.

REMEMBRANCE OF LOVE

Cathie Linz

A CANDLELIGHT ECSTASY ROMANCE™

Published by
Dell Publishing Co., Inc.
1 Dag Hammarskjold Plaza
New York, New York 10017

Dell ® TM 681510, Dell Publishing Co., Inc.

Candlelight Ecstasy Romance™ is a trademark of
Dell Publishing Co., Inc., New York, New York.

ISBN: 0-440-17297-7

Printed in the United States of America
First printing—April 1982

Dear Reader:

In response to your continued enthusiasm for Candlelight Ecstasy Romances™, we are increasing the number of new titles from four to six per month.

We are delighted to present sensuous novels set in America, depicting modern American men and women as they confront the provocative problems of modern relationships.

Throughout the history of the Candlelight line, Dell has tried to maintain a high standard of excellence to give you the finest in reading enjoyment. That is and will remain our most ardent ambition.

Anne Gisonny
Editor
Candlelight Romances

For C. R.

CHAPTER ONE

Karyn was sitting on the lower deck, enjoying the fresh sea breeze and the beautiful turquoise water, her sun hat and dark glasses protecting her from the brilliant glare, when she heard someone behind her ask, "Is this chair taken?"

Her heart stopped and her cheeks paled. It couldn't be the same man. She turned her head to see a tall, slender, masculine figure lower himself onto the deck chair next to hers.

"Are you all right?" he inquired. "You look like you've seen a ghost."

Karyn just stared at him. The same dark brown hair and bright blue eyes set in a tanned face molded by high cheekbones. The same lines next to a sensuously curved mouth made to laugh, and love. Christopher Reid, her missing husband!

How she had loved him. Had it been only a year ago that she'd fulfilled her fantasy of marrying the man she loved? Theirs had been a quiet ceremony with only a few close friends and relatives attending. It had taken place on a beautiful sunny day in her hometown of Lincoln, Nebraska, in the park next to a lake, with a justice of the peace presiding. They had had a short reception afterwards at a small exclusive restaurant and then left early to fly to Chicago. From there they were going on to London for an extended two-month honeymoon, exploring the English countryside. Their overseas flight departed the next morning, so they had checked into a first class hotel for the night's layover.

Karyn had been in the bathroom preparing herself for this long awaited night when the phone had rung in the bedroom. Christopher's voice was barely discernible through the bathroom door as he answered it. Taking a deep breath and a last look in the mirror to check her appearance, Karyn opened the door to the bedroom to find her new husband hanging up the phone, a worried expression on his face. She immediately knew something was wrong.

"Christopher, what is it?"

"I have to go out for a few hours. It's an emergency."

"Is it your uncle?" Karyn knew that both his parents had been killed in an auto accident six years before, and that, with the exception of his uncle, he had no immediate family.

"No, it's not my uncle."

"Then who was it?"

"I'm not at liberty to say, it's not my secret to reveal," he said in a quiet, strained voice.

"Do you mean to tell me that you're leaving me on our honeymoon night without a word of explanation as to why or where you're going?" she demanded.

"You'll have to trust me. You know I wouldn't leave you unless it was a real emergency."

She sank onto the bed, trying to understand what was happening. How could Christopher think of leaving her at a time like this? And why was he being so secretive?

"You're going now?"

"I'll be back in three or four hours at the most," Christopher assured her.

"Do you promise?" Karyn whispered, suddenly afraid.

"Cross my heart and   "

Karyn's hand covered his mouth before he could recite

8

the rest of the well-known saying. "Don't finish it. I'll wait for you."

His blue eyes darkened to a deep indigo. "Thank you." He bent down to give her a fiery kiss before he let himself out the door.

Six hours later it was getting light outside and there was still no sign of Christopher. In desperation she called the police to see if he had been involved in an accident; but Chicago is a large city and, as far as the district officer could tell, no one answering Christopher's description had been reported in an accident in the immediate area. Twelve hours later she called the university where Christopher worked and then his best friend, Michael. It had been humiliating to phone the morning after her wedding to ask if they'd seen her husband. Most of them had been sympathetic; all proved unhelpful. A few of them had kidded her, "Lost him already?"

After trying everyone she could think of with no success, she called the police to report him as a missing person. They were no help at all. Their attitude seemed to be that Christopher had left because he wanted to, but they would fill out the appropriate forms for the record and promptly file them away. Missing husbands were not a high priority problem. After speaking to them, Karyn hung up and burst into tears. Alone in a strange city, not knowing what to do or where to turn, she was overcome by a desperate need to speak to someone familiar, so she called her parents.

Mrs. Kadik answered the phone. "Karyn, is that you? I thought your flight for London left an hour ago."

Karyn had forgotten all about their plane reservations in her anxiety about her husband's disappearance.

"There's been a problem," she began.

"With your flight?" her mother broke in.

"No, with Christopher.

"Don't tell me you've had a fight already. You haven't even been married twenty-four hours."

"Mother, we didn't fight. Christopher has disappeared!"

"He's what?"

"Disappeared!"

"Maybe he just stepped out to get a newspaper or something while you were asleep. He'll be back in a few mintues. Why, I remember the time your father . . ."

"Christopher didn't disappear this morning," Karyn interrupted. "He's been missing since eleven last night. He got a phone call. He told me it was an emergency and that he would have to leave for a few hours."

"Where did he say he was going?"

"That's just it, he said he couldn't tell me."

"You mean Christopher left without even telling you where he was going?" her mother asked in amazement.

"He promised he'd be back."

"He obviously hasn't kept that promise, has he? Have you called the police? Perhaps he was mugged or something."

"Yes, I called the police six hours ago to check that. When I called them to report him as a missing person, they acted as if Christopher was gone because he chose not to return."

There was a heavy pause. "Well, that is a possibility. After all, some men have been known to get cold feet after they've gotten married. You know, all that added responsibility and the permanency of it. It is an adjustment. Maybe he had to go off somewhere for a while and get himself sorted out."

"He wouldn't do that to me and not call to tell me he was all right," she insisted.

"You know there were stories, Karyn. I tried to tell you before you got married, but you wouldn't hear a word against Christopher. It's not as if he were a young boy.

He's twenty-eight, an extremely handsome man who has been a lot of places and known a lot of women."

How did her mother always manage to say the wrong thing? It had been a terrible mistake to call her for comfort. At twenty-five, Karyn was only three years younger than Christopher. Referring to the difference in their ages only succeeded in undermining Karyn's already shaky self-confidence.

"Mother, I've got to go," she said desperately. "He may be trying to call me; I've got to keep the line clear."

"Karyn, wait. Do you want me to fly up and stay with you? I was going to go to a committee meeting, but if you need me, of course I'd cancel that."

"No, Mother, I'll be all right. You go ahead to your meeting, but please don't tell anyone about this."

Mrs. Kadik protested. "You know I wouldn't say anything."

"Yes, well I'll call you if there's any news. Good-bye, Mother."

Karyn hung up feeling worse than before she'd placed the call. Her mother's words had germinated seeds of doubt, possibilities that hadn't occurred to her. What if her mother was right? What if Christopher had panicked and found he couldn't cope with the responsibilities of marriage? No, something inside of her refused to believe that Christopher had deserted her. He'd be back in a few hours with a perfectly reasonable explanation and kiss away her foolish fears.

But Christopher hadn't come back. Not in a few hours or in a few days. Karyn had packed their belongings after extending her stay in the hotel another three days in case he should try to contact her. Even when she left, she gave the man at the front desk her forwarding address at a cheaper hotel. After a week she called in a private detective, but was only able to pay his high fees for a few days,

11

and he had not turned up any additional information. Christopher had simply disappeared into thin air.

Before they were married he was living on campus at the university, and the apartment they were going to move into after their honeymoon wasn't available for another two months, when they were scheduled to return from England. Karyn had no choice but to return to her parents' house.

The realization that Christopher was not coming back didn't hit her immediately. Those first weeks after she got home retained a nightmarish quality, a disassociation with reality. Karyn lost weight—she couldn't eat or sleep. Dark circles ringed the haunted pools of her eyes. After a time her system was forced to apply its own anesthesia, and she became numb, frozen in a state of suspended animation.

She couldn't face staying in the same town, seeing the sympathetic smiles and hearing the curious whispers whenever she went past. The letter from her best friend, Susan, inviting Karyn to come stay with her in Seattle, was the answer to a prayer. She needed to get away. In new surroundings Karyn gradually recovered enough to be able to go through at least the motions of living.

She got a job as a secretary in a lawyer's office. In her free time she kept to herself. Her natural warmth and generosity were locked up behind a wall of habitual reserve. It was a solitary existence, but it was a placid one and after her traumatic experience with Christopher, tranquillity was what she needed. Love had been a harsh teacher, and Karyn learned her lesson well. Under no circumstances would she ever let anyone hurt her like that again.

After working for a year, Karyn was given two weeks vacation. She planned on spending the time in Bermuda after Susan, who had spent a holiday there a few years ago, raved about it.

"Bermuda is off the coast of North Carolina, not in the

Caribbean like the other islands. It's very clean and has an atmosphere all its own. Great place to relax, safe to go out alone with no one hassling you."

That was important to Karyn because she didn't want any men involved in her life. She didn't trust them and had bitterly decided that life was much smoother without them. Her vows to stay aloof and unattached were not hard to maintain.

So Karyn had landed in Bermuda three days ago and taken this island cruise tour today, never dreaming she'd meet the husband who had disappeared into thin air a thousand miles and long ago.

"Do you need help?" his voice jerked her back into the present.

"Christopher?" she croaked. After all, there were such things as look-alikes. Perhaps this was the case.

He looked surprised and then a little ill at ease.

"Yes, my name is Christopher," he said slowly. "Perhaps we should go into the lounge where we can speak privately."

In shock, Karyn followed him into the small empty lounge at the back of the ship. The rest of the passengers were enjoying the sunshine on the top deck.

Christopher sat down and looked out the small porthole.

"I was involved in an accident about a year ago," he began. "I'm afraid I've lost my memory." At her surprised look he went on. "Oh, I remember some things, like my name and profession. But not friend's faces or people's names, which has proved to be rather embarrassing. I was visiting Chicago from Milwaukee, where I was living at the time, when I was involved in a hit-and-run accident. I stayed in the hospital for a few weeks and there, by a stroke of luck, one of the nurses recognized me and told me my name and where I lived. She was moving back to

13

Milwaukee herself so she took me up and showed me my apartment. Apparently I'd just gotten back in town after being abroad and hadn't gotten a job yet. You're the first person I've met since then who recognized me. You did know me before, didn't you?" he queried.

As Christopher turned to look at her closely, a ray of sunshine came through the porthole lighting the planes of her face and adding a glow to her auburn hair. His hand reached out to remove her disguising dark glasses and sun hat. Studying her intently, a fleeting memory came through the mists at the back of his mind.

Yes, he recognized those cheekbones and those unusual slanting green eyes. Somewhere in his memory he heard a melodious voice saying, "You'll never forget me, will you?"

"Never," he heard his own voice reassure. "I'd never forget you." Suddenly, Christopher knew who she was.

"Karyn?" he whispered hoarsely. He grabbed her hand and held her trembling fingers in his. "Oh, Karyn, it is you!" he exclaimed in wonder.

She looked into his face to see if she could believe this fantastic tale he had told her. Yes, on his right temple was a small but visible scar that hadn't been there before, and deep scratches marked his right hand. The walls of her carefully built defenses came tumbling down.

"Christopher!" Pulling her hand away from his, she threw her arms around his neck. He gathered her closer, and they sat holding onto each other, trembling, as if they had just come through a dark tunnel and made it safely into the light.

It was some time before either of them was in any condition to speak coherently, and then it was Christopher who whispered, "Didn't I tell you I'd never forget you, my darling wife?"

"But you did forget me until you saw me again. This whole year you've been missing, you never once got in touch with me. I thought it was because you'd discovered that you'd made a mistake and really didn't want the responsibility of being married."

"No, it was never that," Christopher denied vehemently. "The doctors did warn me that my memory could return at any time, that something might jerk it back, a song, a place, or a face. It was your face that brought back the memories and tore away the wall of fog that's been blocking my vision of you." His trembling fingers caressed her anxious features with heartwarming tenderness.

"What on earth have you been doing this year? Are you still living in Milwaukee? And who is this nurse who recognized you?" The questions were quickly fired at him, the last one being the most important to Karyn because Christopher had never lived in Milwaukee. She wanted to know who this woman was who had lied to him.

"Hold on," he laughed unsteadily. "One question at a time. The nurse's name is Stella Dukane and, no, I'm not in Milwaukee any longer. I'm now in Chicago where I've taken over my uncle's business. I did remember my uncle about a month after the accident. Unfortunately, it was too late. I wrote to him, but my letter was answered by his attorney, notifying me that my uncle had died a few weeks earlier and that he had been trying to locate me concerning my uncle's estate. I went and spoke with him about the matter. I knew Uncle Bill had been involved in some sort of consultation business, but I was stunned to discover that it was in computer programming and analysis. It was really amazing, I was now in charge of a firm that was in my field. I moved to Chicago and have been in charge of the firm ever since, about eleven months now."

"And you, what's been happening to you this past year? Are you still in . . ." He paused, a confused frown marring his forehead. "You know, it's the stupidest thing, but I can't seem to remember where you're from. Was it Milwaukee, too?"

Karyn was concerned. "No, I came from Lincoln, Nebraska. We met at the university there."

Christopher accepted that without question. "Are you still in Lincoln?"

"No, I needed a change of pace after . . . after you disappeared, so I moved to Seattle."

"Seattle!" he exclaimed in shock. "But that's on the other side of the continent. What made you pick Seattle?"

"A friend of mine lives there. She helped me settle in and get a job."

"What do you do?"

"I'm a legal secretary," she informed him.

Christopher began rubbing his forehead. "I don't understand. If I met you in Lincoln, what was I doing in Chicago when I had the accident? And why did I go back to Milwaukee afterwards?"

Hearing the note of strain in his voice and seeing the confusion on his face, Karyn realized that she would have to tread carefully until she checked with his physician as to how much of his past life Christopher could safely be made aware of.

"We were in Chicago because we were going to catch a flight to Europe. You went back to Milwaukee afterwards because you'd forgotten the months directly preceding the accident." That much was true, she thought to herself. He'd forgotten that he'd never lived in Milwaukee!

"With you in Seattle and me in Chicago, there's every chance that our paths would never have crossed if we hadn't come to Bermuda. I can't believe we've found each other after all this time."

Karyn nestled closer, scarcely able to believe the miracle herself. Yet the arms encircling her were real enough, as was the heart pounding against hers. They stayed wrapped in each other's arms until a group of passengers came down onto the deck outside the lounge, whereupon

Christopher reluctantly released her. Gazing up at him with radiant green eyes, Karyn asked, "Where are you staying in Bermuda?"

He named a large hotel near Hamilton, the capital.

"That's terribly expensive and doesn't give you a real feel for the island. I'm staying in a guesthouse in St. George. It's got a lovely view of the old harbor and is just a few minutes walk from the center of town. The pace is much slower in St. George; it's like stepping back in time."

"Do you think there would be an extra room at your guesthouse?"

"Extra room?" Karyn questioned.

"For me," he explained.

"I'm sure there would be. Mrs. Robertson was saying just this morning that the tourist season hasn't really started yet and she wasn't filled up . . ."

The surging throb of the boat's engines drowned out the rest of Karyn's statement. Passengers began collecting their belongings while crew members completed their allotted tasks. The flurry of activity was an indication that they would soon be docking in Hamilton. The sightseeing cruise was over.

"As soon as we dock we'll take a cab to my hotel and I'll pack. Then we can catch the bus over to St. George," he suggested.

Karyn waited in the lobby while Christopher went up to his room to pack. He came back down several minutes later and spoke with the receptionist, presumably explaining his sudden departure. The bus trip from Hamilton to St. George took about forty-five minutes. Karyn had a hard time getting adjusted to driving on the left side of the road, a sign of the close ties between Bermuda and Britain.

They left the bustling city of Hamilton behind and were soon on the road that followed the north shore of the island. The coastline here was rockier and rougher than that of the south shore, where pale sandy beaches with

17

protected coves stretched along the coast, but the water was still the brilliant azure peculiar to the tropics. They got off the bus in St. George and walked the one block up Old Maid's Lane, a very narrow alley that was now a one-way street. The Hilltop guesthouse was set back from the street with a colorful garden bordering both sides of the walk. The house itself was old and sturdy, the architecture reminiscent of a southern plantation complete with white columns and a veranda.

There was no problem obtaining a room for Christopher; in fact, it was only three doors down from Karyn's. She nervously sat on the bed in his room where they talked while he unpacked. The practical realities of their reunion were catching up with her. On the surface Christopher didn't appear to have changed much, but once Karyn looked closer she could see the shadows that clouded his blue eyes, the tighter lines of his face. Otherwise he was as charming, easygoing, and self-assured as ever.

"How are we going to proceed from here?" she asked uncertainly.

"I presume you're not asking about the day's itinerary, but rather about the course our relationship should take?" He waited for her nod before continuing. "What would you like to do?"

"I think we should take it slowly at first. After all, we haven't seen each other for a year, and it's normal that it will take a bit of time to get adjusted." She anxiously glanced at him, trying to gauge his reaction to her views. He caught that glance and, correctly interpreting it, sat down next to her on the bed.

"Karyn, I realize that it's not easy for you, and I don't expect to just show up and jump into bed with you as if this past year hadn't divided us. Not that I don't want to," he grinned, the look in his eyes making her bones melt. "We should have this time together to get reacquainted.

18

So let's take each day as it comes and pretend for the time being that we're engaged instead of married, okay?"

"Thank you, Christopher," she murmured gratefully, leaning over to kiss him. As he began to kiss her back, Karyn felt as if she had gone back in time. She certainly didn't need to get used to his caresses; they were exactly as she had remembered and longed for all the time he had been gone. Come to think of it, they were better because this was reality, and she would not be waking up to find she was alone.

Then Karyn stopped thinking as the sweet possession of his lips sent her senses reeling. When he released her mouth to begin an exploring search of her neck, she kept her face upturned, enjoying the magic of his touch. A sigh of longing broke from her lips a moment before he claimed them again in a long, drugging kiss that stole her breath and awakened dormant feelings of passion. Her arms slid around his neck and up through the soft, brown hair that grew low on his nape. Leaning closer to mold herself against his length, she caught him off balance, and they both fell back on the bed.

A desire to be closer still to the straining muscles of his body sent her fingers down over his chest to the buttons of his shirt, slowly releasing them so she could feel the throbbing of his heart. His hand on her body followed the same course hers had taken, around her smooth shoulders and down, whispering across the tip of her breast to rest on her heart. She was hot and shuddering by the time Christopher wrenched his mouth from hers to bury it in her auburn curls.

"Karyn?" His voice was muffled by her hair.

"Mmmm?"

"I think we'd better stop right about here, because if we continue we're going to break our agreement."

She nodded and was reluctantly moving away when his words stopped her.

19

"We've discovered one important thing about our future, Karyn."

She turned her slightly puzzled face toward him. "What's that?"

"Our bodies don't need any time to get reacquainted; they seem to have perfect recall!"

Karyn blushed and got off the bed, smoothing her blue and white striped cotton shirt over her jeans.

"It's getting late. Where would you like to go for dinner?" she asked him, changing the subject.

"Is the Carriage House nearby?"

"Yes, it's just down the road a bit."

"Fine, we'll go there," he decided. "I'll phone for reservations."

"I'll go change."

Christopher turned with the phone in his hand and mouthed, "Your room at seven?" She nodded and, as she closed the door, heard him request a table for two.

Back in her own room Karyn opened the closet door and examined her wardrobe for something suitable to wear. Having read that dining was a fairly formal affair in most of Bermuda's restaurants, she'd brought her black jersey skirt, cut on the bias so that it swirled as she moved, and several fancy silk blouses to go with it. Little had she suspected when she packed for this trip that she would be going to dinner with Christopher, her husband. That word sounded so good. She felt as though she'd been given a chance at a new life. What had happened in the past was a terrible fluke, but they'd found each other again and would have a lovely future, together.

Glancing at her wristwatch, she noted that she'd better get a move on and stop daydreaming or she'd be late. After a quick shower, Karyn dusted a lightly perfumed talcum powder over her slim body and slipped the black skirt over her head before selecting an emerald-green blouse to go with it. The blouse matched the color of her eyes and made

20

them glow. Maybe it was Christopher that had made them glow *that* brightly, she thought to herself with a grin!

Her shoulder-length auburn hair was brushed back from its center part and then pinned so that the curls cascaded down over her ears and highlighted her high cheekbones. A touch of emerald eye shadow, mascara, and red lip gloss were all the makeup she needed. Stepping back from the mirror to get an overall look she thought, "Not bad," twirling around so that the skirt flared out from her long legs. Ooops, she'd forgotten her shoes. She sat on the bed and slipped on the narrow-strapped black sandals, but before Karyn could fasten them around her ankles, there was a knock at the door. She jumped up to answer it, forgetting about the loose sandals. As she opened the door, she tripped over them and fell into Christopher's arms.

"Do you greet everyone who knocks on your door this way?" he chuckled, coming in and shutting the door after him.

"No, only the handsome ones!" Karyn answered cheekily.

"I can see I'm going to have to keep my eyes on you, young lady," he scolded.

"Only your eyes?" she retorted.

"Getting bold aren't we?" he drawled before jerking her to him and kissing her warmly. One kiss led to another until Karyn breathlessly pulled away.

"I tripped over my sandals. I was just doing them up when you knocked."

"Allow me," he offered with a princely bow and a teasing glint in his blue eyes. She sat on the bed while Christopher kneeled before her.

"Ah, the slipper fits! Cinderella, you shall be my bride!"

"Fool!" Karyn laughed.

"Fool?" he growled. "You dare call the prince a fool?"

21

He stood up and continued with mock ferocity. "You shall be suitably punished."

Karyn joined in the fun by pretending to tremble in her seat. "Oh, Sire, how shall you punish me?"

Christopher stroked a nonexistent beard. "Hmm, I think a kiss would be suitable. Yes, the maid shall kiss the prince."

Karyn stood up and walked over to him, her head bent in order to keep herself from laughing. She slid her hand up over his smooth cotton shirt, feeling the heat emanating from within. Oh, so slowly she proceeded, her hand continuing up over his throat to his jawline and then his smooth tanned cheeks, her forefinger tracing the outline of his firm lips. Finally she lifted her bowed head to whisper, "I obey, m'lord," and placed her parted lips on his for a fiery kiss. Lambent flames of desire flickered between them.

"You're not Cinderella—you're a witch," he muttered against her lips, before moving to nibble her earlobe.

"Oh, Christopher! I'm so glad I found you again." Karyn hugged him tightly, tears coming to her eyes as she realized how improbable their meeting had been.

"You're crying," Christopher accused gently. With his finger he carefully wiped the lonely teardrop from her cheek and, licking it off his fingertip, he grinned. "Umm, not bad, but a little salty."

A watery smile curved her lips. "Let's go eat."

The Carriage House restaurant was located in the Carriage Museum, well-known for its unique collection of old Bermuda carriages. The headwaiter directed them to a lantern-lit table overlooking St. George's Harbour. The orange directing lights from Bermuda's Civil Airport were reflected in the smooth, dark waters of the harbor.

After studying the menu, Karyn decided on the Victoria Cut of Prime Rib and Christopher ordered the King's Prime Rib. A visit to the extensive salad bar was included with their meal. Karyn thought she had enough room to request a piece of Bavarian chocolate cream pie for dessert, but found she had to enlist Christopher's help in polishing it off.

"Umm," she sighed, wiping her lips with the napkin. "That was delicious. I couldn't eat another thing."

"Would you like to take a stroll along the wharf?" he inquired.

"Sounds good," Karyn agreed.

Christopher signaled the waiter and, after paying the bill, they were off. Walking along the waterfront, admiring the many sailing sloops docked there, it was easy to fantasize about the crossings these ships must've had. Their origins were varied, one of them displayed the flag of Canada, while another had the flag of Germany. The air turned chilly, so Christopher dropped his jacket over her shoulders. It was still warm from his body and smelled like his aftershave. He slipped his arm around her shoulder, and they strolled back toward Somers Wharf, stopping to look in the shop windows.

"What do you think of your first day in St. George?" Karyn asked. "Do you feel the different atmosphere that I described? . . . Of stepping back in history when life wasn't so hurried and harried?"

"Yes, I do feel it. Especially at night. Hamilton is really hopping in the evenings, while here things are calm and peaceful. Although, they do seem to be restoring parts of town," Christopher noted, indicating the beautiful shops and restaurants in the newly renovated Somers Wharf waterfront complex.

They slowly made their way back to their guesthouse, enjoying the crisp night air. Stopping outside her door, Karyn couldn't bring herself to say the words that would end the evening. A gentle tug and she was in his arms, pliantly yielding to Christopher's searching kiss. Excitement raced through her veins at the magic of his touch.

Involuntarily, she pressed closer to his lean length. His kiss deepened as he felt her warm response. His hands moved along her back, around to her waist, and then higher where they began a sensuous exploration of her softly rounded curves.

Karyn turned her head away while she still had the will to do so. She was trembling, his pervading desire forging an identical yearning deep within her. His lips moved caressingly over her temples and the heated contours of her cheeks. The electrical intensity of their responses wasn't easy to switch off. Christopher slowly lifted his head and framed her face with his slightly trembling fingers, while Karyn gazed up at him. He seemed to get an immense amount of satisfaction out of just looking at her. Karyn felt the same way about him. Bending down, he brushed her lips with his.

"Breakfast at eight?"

She nodded.

"Good night, my love," he whispered, eyes moving over her in a touching caress. She caught his hand as he turned to move away.

"You . . . you will be here in the morning, won't you?" she asked hesitantly, needing his reassurance.

"Want me to prove it?" he grinned, moving back toward her.

"You just did," she smiled gratefully. "Good night."

CHAPTER TWO

Karyn awoke with a pleasant sense of well-being that was reflected by the sweet smile on her lips. As she lay in bed, a bar of sunshine came through the window and rested on the gold band of her wedding ring. With it came the recollection of why she was so happy: she and Christopher were reunited again! Jumping out of bed, she ran to the dresser where she had left her watch the night before. It was early yet, only a little after six. She'd slept well the previous night, surprising herself, because she thought she might be too excited to sleep.

Since it was such a lovely morning, Karyn decided to get dressed and sit out in the yard, enjoying the view. Not knowing what she and Christopher would be doing that day, she decided to play it safe and wear her jeans again with a bright-red cotton T-shirt. The outfit could always be changed if it wasn't suitable. She combed her auburn curls into a ponytail at the back of her head and walked out the door, taking only her key since she wasn't going far.

Outside, the island was coming to life with a symphony of sounds. A slender palm rustled majestically, then a burst of birdsong was added, punctuated by a barking dog. The soft breeze teasing Karyn's hair held a touch of saltiness reminiscent of the open sea. Early morning's special magic was everywhere.

When Karyn reached the front of the house, she

stopped suddenly at the sight of a lonely figure leaning against the stone wall surrounding the garden. It wasn't until she walked closer that she realized it was Christopher. Putting her hand on his arm, she murmured his name and felt his startled jerk, as if he had been a million miles away.

"What are you doing up so early?" he asked her.

Not quite the greeting she would have hoped for, but then, she had startled him while he was obviously deep in thought.

"It's such a beautiful morning, I thought I'd come watch the town waking up. How about you?"

"I came out to think, to try and fit the pieces of the puzzle together." Karyn's hand slid down his arm to curl around his fingers, offering what comfort she could. "All I come up with are more questions. Why didn't you look for me in Milwaukee? Why did I leave you in the first place? What was I doing walking the streets of Chicago in the middle of the night? Damn it, why can't I remember?" He snapped out the questions with harsh self-accusation, shaking his head in anger and frustration at the lack of answers. His iron grip on her hand was squeezing the blood from her fingers, but Karyn didn't complain.

The first euphoria of their meeting was beginning to wear off and the questions about the reasons for their separation were coming to the fore.

"Christopher, we obviously need to talk about what happened and help each other as best we can. In the excitement yesterday, we only went into the bare outlines of what occurred. Let's eat something first and then we can go somewhere quiet to talk, perhaps the Botanical Gardens?"

Christopher nodded in agreement, then lifted his hand to look at his watch, keeping her fingers intertwined with his.

"It's a little after seven now, do you know when breakfast is served?

"Yes, between seven and ten."

They stood by the wall a little longer and then she tugged his hand to remind him that they should be moving. Hands clasped, they turned and walked up the path to the front door with its stained-glass window. Inside, Karyn directed Christopher upstairs to the breakfast room. Apparently, they were the first arrivals, but the tables were set in preparation for the morning guests. As soon as they sat down, Mrs. Robertson's brother, who helped her each morning, came out of the kitchen with two small glasses of orange juice. After setting a glass at each of their places, Mr. Trent asked, "How would you like your eggs this morning?"

Karyn answered first. "Scrambled, please."

"Sunny-side up," Christopher requested.

"Coffee?"

"No, thank you, not for me." She turned inquiringly to Christopher.

"Yes, I could use a cup this morning," he decided.

Christopher waited until Mr. Trent had returned to the kitchen before asking Karyn how they would get to the Botanical Gardens.

"There must be a bus. Just a minute." She got up and walked over to a small end table where she picked up several fliers and brochures before returning to her seat.

"I remembered Mrs. Robertson saying she kept information from the tourist office and that if we wanted one to just help ourselves. So I did," she explained.

"You sure did!" Christopher agreed, looking at the pile of brochures in front of him.

"I only took half of the ones available," Karyn defended herself while unfolding the flier marked PUBLIC TRANSPORTATION BERMUDA. Laying the map out on the table in front of them, she pointed with a slender finger.

27

"We're here and the Botanical Gardens are . . ." She paused to study the map—"down here"—pointing to the area southeast of Hamilton. "That means we would take the Number Eight bus to Grotto Bay and then change to a Number Two. That should take us there."

"Fine. How often does the bus leave St. George? And how about connections?"

"Oh, the bus in St. George is no problem, it leaves every fifteen minutes. But I don't see a connection listed for the Number Two bus."

"Perhaps we should ask Mrs. Robertson." Christopher sounded gently amused.

"Good idea," Karyn agreed, folding up the map as Mr. Trent came in with their plates. Several slices of crisp bacon and four pieces of toast accompanied their eggs. While Christopher was sipping his second cup of coffee, Mrs. Robertson came out of the kitchen to inquire after her guests' well-being and their plans for the day.

"We'd like to go to the Botanical Gardens, but aren't sure of the bus route," Karyn explained.

"You picked a hard place to get to by bus," Mrs. Robertson laughed. "Let's see." She bent over the map. "Yes, that's the best route to take. Have you got it?" she asked after drawing several lines and circles with her pen.

Looking at Karyn's uncertain face, Christopher answered for them both. "Thank you, Mrs. Robertson. We'll manage."

"I hope we can," Karyn whispered after their hostess had moved on to another table.

"If in doubt, we can always get a cab," he pointed out.

"We'd better be on our way to our great adventure."

They left the room, saying good-bye to the other guests as they went. Mrs. Robertson liked her guests to be friendly, and since it was a small guesthouse, that wasn't hard to do.

Karyn and Christopher made their way to their separate rooms, agreeing to meet fifteen minutes later by the front door. Back in her room, Karyn freshened up. Looking into the mirror, she suddenly felt in need of a little boost to her morale. Some plum eye shadow and a touch of lipstick improved the picture somewhat. The ponytail made her look younger than her twenty-six years, but there was no time to change it.

Karyn picked up her purse, checking for her money and room key before grabbing her camera at the last minute. Christopher was just coming from his room as she walked into the hallway, so she waited for him. Together they walked outside into the sunshine where the light was so bright that Karyn was immediately forced to dig into her purse for her sunglasses. Christopher, she noticed, had already donned a pair. As they walked down Old Maid's Lane he asked about its unusual name.

"I read something about it in one of these brochures." She reached into her purse and pulled one out. "Yes, this is it. Let's see . . ." When the pertinent paragraph was found, Karyn began to read: " 'It is the proud boast of St. George that it is the oldest continuous Anglo-Saxon settlement in the New World, having been founded in 1612. Jamestown was settled five years earlier, but Bermudians point out that the first Virginians had to abandon their colony. St. George has been inhabited ever since its founding, although it fell asleep when the capital was moved to Hamilton in 1815. Careful restoration is being carried out so that St. George's past atmosphere will be brought back to life. Even the street names conjure up images of its past, names like One Gun Alley, Featherbed Alley,' " she paused as Christopher laughed, " 'and Old Maid's Lane, originally called Duke of Cumberland Lane. Unlike Williamsburg, virtually all the seventeenth- and eighteenth-century buildings here are original . . . .' " Karyn completed her narrative just as they arrived at the main street in

29

St. George, the Duke of York Street, where they caught the bus.

About an hour and several confusing bus connections later, they arrived at the Botanical Gardens. The flowerbeds were artistically arrayed, with a spectrum of colors displayed in each one. Strolling by, Karyn was able to recognize some snapdragons and delphiniums, but the majority were unfamiliar to her. An informative sign stated that there were 950 different kinds of flowering trees, plants, and vines on the island. The horticultural beauty was irresistibly photogenic, and she took several pictures, including one of Christopher. They walked on until they found a bench in a quiet corner of the gardens where they sat down.

Karyn took a deep breath and started. "When we met yesterday on the boat, we were so excited, and it was such a shock that we didn't really go into much detail about our separation. I was overjoyed to find you. The details didn't matter, as long as we were together again. Last night was like stepping back in time to when we were engaged—the laughter and the loving. But this morning the questions have come back, and we've got to face them together. Agreed?"

"Agreed," Christopher nodded. "Since the problem is with me, I guess I'll start."

Karyn winced at his bitter use of the word *problem*.

He continued: "The thrill of finding you temporarily replaced my frustration at not being able to remember the past. For a while I no longer cared that the pieces didn't fit. The past was there, but just out of reach when I grabbed for it. I knew that you were my wife and that I loved you. I also knew that something had happened and that somehow I'd left you. But for what reason, I don't know. Do you?" he turned to ask her.

"No . . . well, sort of," she corrected herself. "You got a telephone call while I was in the other room and told me

30

it was an emergency and that you had to leave for a few hours. That was the last time I saw you," she said with a catch in her voice, "until yesterday on the boat. I called the police when you didn't return, but Chicago is a large city, and they weren't very helpful. Their attitude was, 'Lady, if you lost your husband, he wants to stay lost.' They were supposed to check the lists of injured in area hospitals to see if you'd been involved in an accident."

The lines around Christopher's lips deepened, lending him an unnatural grimness. "I was taken to a hospital in a suburb north of the city," he explained. "That's probably why they weren't able to locate me in the Chicago hospitals."

Karyn could see the effort it took him to talk about the experience. It was written on his face—reflected in the stormy darkness of his eyes. Christopher's absorption was such that she could feel him concentrating, striving to get a fix on the elusive past. His tanned forehead was furrowed, as if in pain.

"Christopher, you can't force your memory to come back to you," she cautioned, concern coloring her soft voice.

"God, I can't even remember sleeping with you!" The words were torn from him.

Karyn was relieved that in this, at least, she would be able to reassure him. She brought their clasped hands up to the hollow between her breasts and held his hand against her heart. "Your accident was on our honeymoon night and you left before we did sleep together," she reminded him. "It wasn't because of a fight," Karyn assured him as she felt his arm tense against her. "We were just getting ready for bed when the call came and you left."

She felt the shudder of relief that went through his body. His voice was husky when he spoke. "After you left last night, I started thinking about your view that we should wait until we got reacquainted before we sleep together. Then it occurred to me that I didn't even know if we had ever made love. I couldn't believe that I would have forgotten something as important to me as that, but then I forgot you until I saw you again, and I suppose I lost confidence in my memory."

Karyn then realized that while she harbored fears about his leaving her again, Christopher felt guilty about forgetting her in the first place. To tell him of her fears would only increase his guilt, and that was something she couldn't do to him.

The conversation had to be steered to smoother waters. "What do you remember about us? Do you know how we met?"

"It's still not very clear to me," he said apologetically. "You said yesterday that we met at the university in Lincoln, Nebraska. I remember the first time I saw you: you were sitting behind a desk, and I thought you were the prettiest thing I'd seen in a long time."

Karyn had to laugh at that. "I'm not sure that's such a great compliment!" Noting Christopher's puzzled look, she went on to explain. "You were finishing your master's degree and I was a secretary in the Computer Science Department. Most of the things in your line of vision were square and had to be programmed." Her humor brought a smile to his lips.

"What else do you remember?" Karyn probed.

"I remember meeting your parents. I don't think your mother liked me very much. Your father was wrapped up in his own world, but we got along quite well. I remember asking you to marry me. It was Christmas. We were walking in the countryside when it began snowing."

Christopher paused as a memory seemed to be beckoning him. He closed his eyes and saw the snowflakes falling from the sky like bits of cotton, saw the two of them frolicking in the snow. He could hear the voices as he stepped back in time to that Christmas.

"Would you like working for me?" he heard his voice saying.

"Do you need a secretary?" she had questioned.

"No, not quite."

"Do you need clerical help, or are you talking about programming?"

"No, I'm talking about a wife."

He remembered that Karyn's face had seemed to glow as she leaned over to kiss him and say, "The salary and fringe benefits seem pretty good, so I think I'll take the job!"

"Christopher!" Karyn's concerned voice brought him back to the present.

"I remembered the whole scene clearly in my mind just now," he announced.

Surely this was an encouraging sign. "That's great! You see, if you take the time and don't push it, things will come back to you. Even if you don't remember all the details of our courtship, you do remember the basics, and that's more than a lot of men can say without your good excuse!" she kidded him.

It was reassuring to know that he was familiar with their romance and remembered asking her to marry him. Now the only questions left were concerning that fateful day, their wedding day.

Christopher must've been reading her mind for he said, "The remaining questions seem to center around that last day, our wedding day. I do recall getting married quite clearly now. I can't see how I could've forgotten it after the accident," he worried, reinforcing Karyn's belief that he was feeling a lot of guilt over not remembering her.

"We were married in a park near a lake, right?" She nodded at his questioning glance. "We went to André's for the reception afterwards. There weren't many people there—just your family and a few mutual friends." He paused a minute, his forehead creased in concentration.

33

"Michael was there!" he exclaimed. "He was my best man. Michael O'Hara. You see, I'd forgotten him, too. God knows what else I've forgotten! You don't think I was married before, do you?" he panicked.

"Christopher, you're not being logical," Karyn chided him. "You weren't suffering from amnesia when I met you. You knew everything about your background and family. This past year you've known that you've been suffering from amnesia. It's one of the first things you told me when I recognized you. You probably forgot Michael, because you met him that year at the university, through me, actually. And since all memory of me was blocked out, you would have forgotten Michael as well."

Christopher gave her a relieved smile. "I think I've not only lost my memory this past year but a good deal of my sanity as well. I've found it now that I've found you," and he bent his head to kiss her lips. "I feel like such a heel for not being able to get in touch with you. When I think of what you had to go through this past year, it tears me apart. I can imagine what it must have done to you."

She had to shudder as he brought up her feelings. While she thought about Christopher and his problems, she didn't have time to think about her fears. And that was the way Karyn wanted it. The pain from that period in her life was too intense, the scar too freshly healed to test.

"Tell me what you're thinking," he prompted her.

"I was just going back myself and remembering what it was like when you were gone. I don't think I could ever handle that again!" she broke out.

"You won't ever have to go through that again. If the phone rings after 8:00 P.M., I'm not answering it," he kidded in an attempt to cheer her up.

Karyn smiled appreciatively and asked, "Have I told you today how much I love you?"

Christopher pretended to consider the question for a minute and then replied, "No, not to the best of my recollection. You know I have this memory problem, so you may have to repeat things over and over!"

"What kind of things?" she questioned in mock innocence.

"Things like I love you, I need you, and I want you. And actions, too, like this." He demonstrated by pulling her into his arms, kissing both her eyelids, then her cheeks and nose, before he finally reached her mouth. His kiss had a teasing quality that changed, at her response, into a long and lingering caress.

"Karyn," he sighed her name.

"Yes?" Her lips were warm against his throat.

"Just Karyn," he smiled, resting his chin on the top of her head. His deft fingers loosened the clasp fastening her ponytail and combed through the silken mass of her auburn hair.

The sound of footsteps on the path interrupted their warm embrace. Karyn pulled away, embarrassed at being caught in such a public spot. When she tried to tidy her hair Christopher grabbed her hand and kissed each of her fingers with soul-shattering tenderness.

"You look lovely just as you are," he commented huskily.

A becoming blush stained her cheeks. "Are you sure?" she asked uncertainly. "I don't look . . ." She floundered for a minute, trying to find the right word.

"Wanton," Christopher suggested helpfully, devilish amusement glinting in his dark blue eyes.

"No!" Karyn's blush increased as she smoothed her hair in confusion. "I don't, do I?" she asked anxiously, then heard his responding chuckle.

"You tease!"

"That's not a tease," he corrected.

"Oh? Then what is a tease?"

Christopher leaned towards her, not stopping until his lips brushed hers. "I'll show you later," he promised against them. Then he stood up and smiled down into her bemused face. "Let's go for a walk."

Grabbing one of her hands, he pulled her up next to him and headed back toward the main path of the garden. They strolled silently for nearly an hour, just enjoying the flowers, sunshine, and company, although not necessarily in that order.

"I'm getting hungry, what time is it?" Karyn asked.

Christopher glanced down at his watch. "It's just after one. What happened to your watch? You had it last night."

"I left it on the sink in my room this morning. It isn't waterproof," she explained.

"Not like our love," he countered in a conversational tone of voice.

"What?" Karyn looked at him in surprise.

"Our love is unbreakable, shockproof, dustproof, and waterproof."

"If it's waterproof, that means we can take it swimming with us," she teased.

"That's a good idea, but I don't think this is quite the place," Christopher added, his blue eyes dancing as his hand indicated the flowerbeds surrounding them.

"A little dry," Karyn agreed. "But we could go back to our rooms and change, then catch the shuttle up to the pool," and she named the large hotel on the hill above St. George.

Christopher confirmed that that sounded like a good idea, so they set off to catch the next bus back to St. George.

Once back in her room at the Hilltop, Karyn stripped off her clothes and put on her swimsuit. The black one-piece suit was made of a lycra material that clung to her body like a second skin. Standing there critiquing her appearance in the mirror she decided that the swimsuit certainly accentuated what lay underneath it. She felt a

36

slight twinge of embarrassment at the thought of Christopher seeing her like this.

The suit was new; she'd bought it expressly for this trip. But somehow, back in the ill-lit dressing room of the boutique where she'd bought it in Seattle, it hadn't looked so, well, sexy, she thought to herself. As she turned sideways to see how the material faithfully followed her curves, she realized that Christopher had never seen her in a swimsuit before. They'd met in September and, while Indian summer comprised some warm days, none of them had been warm enough for swimming. They'd been married in May and, after his disappearance, she hadn't seen him again until yesterday, again in May, only a year later.

Realizing that she had come close to using up her allotted time, Karyn stepped into her jeans and pulled a loose blue, bat-sleeve top over her head. Putting her purse in her beach bag she checked for her towel and left her room.

When she met Christopher at the front door, he looked much the same as when she had left him a half hour earlier. He still wore his dark blue jeans that tightly molded his masculine form and a light-blue short-sleeve cotton shirt with the first few buttons undone. As she got closer, a smile came to her lips when she recalled some of the lawyers at the office picnic the previous summer. Most of the men seemed to think that having their shirts undone all the way down to their waists with their hairy chests hung with chains really made them look like "macho men"; but Karyn had thought they looked ridiculous.

Christopher was much more to her liking: He had enough sex appeal and self-confidence that he didn't need to flaunt anything. He was potent enough as it was, she thought, glancing at his tan throat rising from his collar. Lifting her eyes, she again appreciated his lean good looks —the clean-cut square jaw, the firm mouth with its slightly fuller lower lip, the high cheekbones leading up to his eyes. She could get quite dreamy just about those eyes.

They were a brilliant blue oasis in his tanned face, turning a deep indigo, depending on his mood.

Christopher, catching her staring at him, tilted his head quizzically. "Did I leave something undone?"

"What?"

"You were fixing me with such an intense stare that I wondered if something was wrong!"

"Nothing's wrong," she assured him. "I was just admiring your good looks." She was surprised to see a slight wave of red appear under his tanned cheeks.

"Let's get going before we miss the shuttle," he muttered, hurrying out the door. As Karyn followed him, she was amazed to discover that she had actually embarrassed her husband by complimenting him on his handsome features. She had a feeling she'd be in the same boat when Christopher saw her in her swimsuit!

A hotel shuttle bus left from the center of town every few minutes, taking guests up the sharply winding road to the large hotel situated on the crest of the hill overlooking St. George. It was a short ride—only about ten minutes. Karyn felt guilty about not walking the distance until she turned and noticed how full the bus was. Apparently she wasn't the only one who felt lazy today.

Once at the pool area they paid the small fee charged to nonguests for the use of the hotel pool and went toward the changing rooms. Luckily there wasn't a mirror there, so Karyn didn't have to face her reflection, giving her second thoughts. She couldn't stay in the room forever. It's not as if the suit were some skimpy shoestring bikini like some of the other guests were half-wearing, she tried to reassure herself.

Taking a deep breath, she opened the door and slung her beach bag over her shoulder. Karyn didn't pause to look around for Christopher until she reached a quiet poolside corner. As she put her hand up to shield her eyes from the glaring sun, she felt a smooth finger run down her spine, left bare by the low back of her suit. She jerked in surprise before she heard Christopher's reassuring voice near her ear, his breath ruffling the curls by her cheek.

"It's only me. You don't think I'd let anyone else touch you like that, do you?" he queried.

"Oh, I didn't see you," Karyn stuttered.

He slid his warm hand back up her spine, over her shoulder and down her arm, giving her goose bumps and sending waves of insidious pleasure through her body.

"Why, you're shivering," Christopher noted with concern. "Are you cold?" He reached for her other hand.

Shaking her head, she threw him a challenge. "Last one in the pool is a rotten egg!"

She had almost made it to the edge of the pool when Christopher swooped up from behind, hoisted her up in his arms, and jumped into the water with her. As they sank, their limbs intertwined, he put his lips to hers in a passionate kiss that didn't stop until they were both breathless and had to surface for air. When they broke the surface, Karyn nervously glanced around, trying to see if anyone had noticed their tumultuous embrace.

"That was to show my appreciation of your appearance in that swimsuit," Christopher informed her. "It even feels as good as it looks," he continued, his actions demonstrating his meaning as he molded the palms of his hands across the smooth material where it tightly stretched over her curvaceous body.

"Christopher!" she protested, her breath coming out in short erratic gasps.

"I couldn't help myself," he claimed, hanging his head in a mock show of contrition.

They splashed around for a few minutes and then Karyn, feeling the warm sun on her shoulders, decided to get out of the pool and go back to their lounge chairs to put on some sunscreen. Christopher waved as she got out and then turned on his stomach and did a smooth crawl stroke, which he steadily kept up for several laps across the pool.

Karyn looked up some time later to see and feel him dripping over her.

"I think I'm waterlogged; my fingers look like prunes!" He held them out for her inspection.

"I always knew you were fruity!" she exclaimed.

"I thought I was nutty," he countered, dropping into the lounge chair beside her.

"Then why don't you rub a little of this on," Karyn advised, handing him the tube of sunscreen with coconut oil. "If you're going to be nutty, you might as well smell the part!"

Christopher took the proffered tube and began rubbing the brown ointment into his skin. After greasing all the areas he could easily reach, he turned to Karyn for assistance with those he could not. She obligingly squeezed a worm-shaped gob of ointment onto the palm of her hand and began rubbing it into the already tanned surface of his back.

Her fingers moved over the rippling muscles, enjoying the feel of him. His skin was still slightly cool from the water in the pool. This close, she noticed the way his thick, dark hair was a little uneven at the edges, as if he hadn't had it cut for a while. His skin was warming from the sun now, and as she continued the kneading movements of her hands, she felt a growing desire to feel more of him than just his smooth back. Startled by the suddenness of her thoughts Karyn removed her hands as if they'd been burned.

Christopher turned his head over his shoulder to complain, "Umm, that felt good. Why'd you stop?"

She risked one look into his lazy blue eyes before lowering her own, afraid they might reflect her desires.

"My arms got tired," she lamely explained and settled back into her chair, feeling the need to retreat to a safer distance. The capped tube of sunscreen was dropped onto the towel between them. Closing her eyes, Karyn rearranged herself in a more comfortable position. A moment later her eyes flew open again as she felt the lounge creak under Christopher's weight. He was sitting on the side of her chair, holding the discarded sunscreen tube in his hand.

"My turn," he calmly announced.

"What?"

"Turn on your side so I can reach your back."

"No, that's all right, I—I'll manage."

Meeting his uncompromising look Karyn sighed and turned on her side, willing herself not to let the indefinable longings coursing through her get the upper hand. At first she held herself stiffly, but as his warm hands molded her skin, she began to relax and enjoy the almost hypnotic effect of his touch.

It seemed all too soon when Christopher suddenly removed his hands and with a brisk, "you'll do," returned to his seat. His rather abrupt leave-taking gave Karyn cause to wonder if he had become prey to the same sudden urges that she had experienced. As she considered the idea, a light smile curved her lips. She was glad not to be the only one subject to unexpected desires!

They sat soaking up the sunshine for what was left of the afternoon, the warm rays of the sun having a somnolent effect. Karyn had been on the verge of falling asleep several times, only to be jerked back by the sound of laughter from the pool. Glancing at her watch, she realized it was almost five o'clock—time to consider getting back to their guesthouse and preparing for dinner. Come to think of it, maybe the last noise that had jerked her awake had been from her stomach, growling protestingly after expending all that energy for swimming and not getting refilled.

She nudged Christopher with her foot, his leg warm from the afternoon sun.

"Christopher?"

"Ummmm?"

"Did you know it's almost five?"

"No," he replied, not opening his eyes.

"I'm hungry," she announced.

That got a response. Turning his head, he slowly opened one eye to give her a deliciously lecherous look. "Hungry for what?"

"Dinner."

"Oh." His face fell with mock disappointment at her answer.

"We should start back to our rooms so we have time to get ready for dinner," she continued.

After gathering her belongings and putting them all in her beach bag, she stood up and made her way to the changing rooms. She was already completely dry from the sun, so it didn't take her too long to change into her jeans and top.

Going to the hotel lobby where they had agreed to meet, Karyn was rather pleased to see that she'd finished dressing before Christopher had. But that pleasure turned to anxiety when there was still no sign of him ten minutes later. She looked up and down the hallway, but didn't see him. It couldn't take him this long to change.

What if Christopher had disappeared again? The mere possibility was sufficient to drain the color from her lovely face. Please God, not again! Blind panic tunneled her vision and quickened her uneven heartbeat. A loose tendril of hair clung to her now damp forehead. Karyn was desperately trying to regain some measure of control when she finally noticed Christopher striding down the hall toward her. Even though she saw his lips forming words as he came nearer, she couldn't hear them for the wave of relief that washed over her. It wasn't until the rushing

42

noise in her head subsided that she began to comprehend what he was saying.

" . . . lock was jammed so I couldn't open the door. It was damned embarrassing standing there pounding on the door until someone got a maintenance man to come, and then they had to take the whole doorknob apart to reach the stupid lock." Noticing her wan looks, Christopher broke off his explanation to ask, "Are you alright?"

She nodded. "You look awfully pale," he continued. "Are you really that hungry? You should have said something earlier. Here, give me that," taking the beach bag from her limp fingers, "and we'll go catch the bus. Maybe we should stop and pick up something to eat." As he spoke, he guided her toward the entrance and out of the hotel.

Karyn was subdued during the short ride back to St. George, intent on keeping her feelings under control until she reached the privacy of her room. Once safely inside, the reaction quickly set in, and she began to shiver uncontrollably. Christopher entered the room just as Karyn sat down. Taking one look at the state she was in, he dropped her forgotten beach bag on a chair and shut the door behind him. Karyn was pulled into his arms and tenderly cradled within their protective circle.

"What is it—are you ill?" She shook her head. Christopher rocked her to and fro, soothing her the best he could, until the worst of the trembling had subsided. Running the fingers of one hand through her silky auburn hair, he bent his head to whisper in her ear.

"Better now?" At her nod he went on. "Something must have upset you. Won't you tell me what it was?" Her hesitation was unmistakable. "Karyn, we have to be completely honest with one another. Things are complicated enough without our trying to read each other's minds. If something troubles either one of us, we should bring it out

43

into the open and discuss it. It probably won't seem so bad with two of us working on it."

Looking up into his serious and concerned face, she realized the wisdom of his words but felt unable to confide her fears to him. They seemed so foolish now, that she was embarrassed at making a mountain out of a molehill. Therefore Karyn attempted to cover up her erroneous assumption that he'd disappeared again.

"It was nothing. I must've just been tired."

She felt him withdraw as she spoke. Dropping his arms from around her, he said coolly, "If you don't want to confide in me, there's no way I can force you. I'm just sorry that you don't have enough confidence in me to feel comfortable telling me what the problem is." His words came closer than he realized to the crux of the matter— her lack of confidence in him, and in herself.

Getting up, Christopher strode toward the door. Opening it, he turned to ask, "Are you still planning on eating dinner with me tonight?"

Karyn threw him a startled look and said, "Yes."

"Since you don't trust me sufficiently to confide in me, I didn't want to be presumptuous in assuming that you would trust me enough to dine with me." His voice held a chilling sarcasm that cut her to the quick. "I'll pick you up at seven thirty." He closed the door firmly after him.

Karyn flung herself on the bed and sobbed into her pillow. Christopher already thought she didn't have enough faith in him to share her feelings and was bitter about that. How could she possibly tell him that her faith was so lacking that she was afraid he would disappear from her life again? She just couldn't do it. Her fears would have to be contained. After all, knowing her weakness was half the battle, wasn't it?

Karyn wiped her tears away. She couldn't blame him for being angry. Christopher had sensed her uncertainties and was disappointed by her refusal to communicate with him. The question was how to prevent him from delving deeper into the real reason for her emotional state.

She lay there for some time, trying to think of a way to convince him of her love. Of course, the first thing that came to mind was becoming his wife in the fullest sense of the word, but Karyn soon dismissed this because she strongly felt that making love should not be used as a means of proving anything. Perhaps if she acted as if the scene this afternoon hadn't occurred, they could recapture the camaraderie and rapport they had enjoyed earlier in the day. Having made this decision, she went to shower and wash her hair.

Wrapping her terry bathrobe around her afterward, Karyn got out her small, travel hair blower and began drying her hair, imagining what she would say to Christopher. Since her hair was inclined to curl on its own, she did not need to do anything else to it except brush the chestnut silkiness until it shone. Surveying her reflection in the mirror, she didn't appreciate the beauty of her slightly tilted green eyes and small, pert nose.

Karyn chose a warm brown eye shadow to complement the outfit she planned on wearing. A dark brown eye pencil outlined the unusual shape of her eyes, and a brown mascara darkened her naturally long lashes. Her chocolate, button-down skirt and a matching silk shirt were pulled out of the closet. After donning both she added a white leather belt. Standing in front of the mirror Karyn applied a cinnamon lip gloss and stood back to appraise the results. Not too bad, she decided.

The evenings tended to get a little chilly, so she got out her warm white shawl. After transferring her wallet and keys into a small white-leather clutch, she slid her feet into dark-brown-leather, high-heeled evening slippers, and then sat down to wait for Christopher. Glancing at her wrist to check the time, she found it bare and realized that she'd left her watch in the bathroom again. Going to retrieve it her actions reminded her of the conversation they had had earlier in the day at the Botanical Gardens, and a pang went through her as she hoped that that rapport would not be too difficult to recapture.

Christopher knocked on her door at exactly seven thirty. He declined her invitation to come in and stood outside waiting while she gathered up her clutch and shawl, then closed the door after her. They walked in silence down the narrow streets until they passed a small park with a few benches where Christopher paused to ask, "Would you mind if we stopped here for a few minutes? I'd like to talk to you before we eat. It shouldn't take long."

Fear coursed through her veins, momentarily stopping her heart. Was he going to tell her that it was all over? Or that he'd remembered why he'd left her on that night so long ago? Karyn sat down next to him on the bench and sternly schooled her features so that they reflected none of her inner turmoil.

Staring out at the surrounding darkness, Christopher began. "I want to apologize for my behavior earlier this evening. I really don't have the right to walk back into your life after a year and demand to know your every thought. I should have realized that it was bound to take time for you to come to trust me and feel completely at ease with me. My only excuse is that we were so close all day, I'd almost forgotten our separation. Forgetting seems to have become a bad habit with me lately," he tacked on bitterly. "All I can say is this, if you want to talk to me about it, I'll be here because I do love you."

Karyn threw her arms around him and pressed herself to his lean length. "And I love you," she whispered against his lips. She felt his taut body relax as his arms gathered her closer to him, if that was possible. She feathered light kisses across his face until his lips caught and held hers in a gentle kiss of immense tenderness. Loath to

46

remove her lips completely from his she murmured her thanks against his mouth. "Thank you, darling, for being so understanding."

He pressed a kiss on the corner of her mouth and reluctantly released her. "We'd better get moving or we'll be late for our dinner reservation. I only meant to stop for a minute; I didn't mean to keep you from your dinner when I know how hungry you are!" reminding her of their conversation by the pool. He stooped to pick up the white shawl, which had slid to the ground, and looping it around her shoulders, pulled her up from the bench into his arms.

"Just one for the road," he said, and his lips met hers ɪn a sweet kiss that ended too soon. Holding hands, they strolled down the street toward the restaurant in St. George. Like the one the night before, it was set along the wharf overlooking St. George. They were shown to a table near wooden French doors that were opened to reveal an inner courtyard with a fountain. After refusing pre-dinner drinks they casually perused the menu.

"What would you like?" Christopher inquired.

"I can't decide between the scallops and the fish platter. What about you?"

"I'll have the fish platter," he decided, closing his menu.

"Well, if you're having that, I'll have the scallops." At his slightly puzzled look she went on to explain. "Then, I'll just taste your fish platter, and you can taste my scallops."

"A bit of musical plates, eh?" Christopher mocked, as the waiter came to take their order. After he left, Karyn turned to admire the layout of the restaurant. The wall they were seated near overlooked the courtyard, while the opposite wall had full-length glass windows facing the harbor. Reflections of the many boats moored there danced upon the dark waters. Out of the corner of her eye she noticed the guitarist stopping at each table to play requests. Her study was interrupted by the waiter bringing their soup.

They'd just finished their meal when the wandering guitarist came to their table.

"Good evening. How was your meal?"

"Fine, thank you," Christopher replied.

"Is there anything I can play for you tonight?"

Christopher looked at Karyn inquiringly. After a moment's pause she decided. "Could you play 'Yesterday'?" naming one of her favorite Lennon and McCartney compositions.

The guitarist looked a little embarrassed. "Gee, I haven't played that for so long, I'm not sure I remember how it goes. But I'll give it a try."

Actually, he did give it a rather good try, and Karyn sat back to enjoy the lyrical music on the guitar. Afterwards, she thanked him, and he moved out to the courtyard.

Turning to Christopher, she remarked, "I couldn't believe he wasn't sure how to play 'Yesterday.' You'd think he'd get a lot of requests for that song. I mean, it's really a classic."

"So is the '1812 Overture'!" he gently mocked. "Why didn't you request that?"

"You know, I never thought of it. Quick, let's call him back for an encore!" She laughingly turned and raised her hand to catch the guitarist's attention. Christopher grabbed her fingers, and raising them to his lips, told her, "Only one request per table, and you used yours up."

"Too bad," Karyn pouted. "Maybe next time."

After they paid the bill, they took a short stroll around King's Square, which was pretty deserted in the evening since most of the tourists had returned to either their cruise ships or Hamilton. They stopped in front of the restored Town Hall and read the plaque describing some of the local history. " 'Named after the patron saint of England, St. George was the capital of Bermuda from

1612 to 1815. Here began the social and political development of Bermuda as a self-governing colony. . . . ' "

They continued their leisurely walk around the square, stopping every now and then to admire the floodlit buildings.

"If it were daytime, I'd take your picture in the pillory," she informed him.

"The what?"

Karyn indicated the small wooden framework in front of them, with holes for the head and hands.

"That's where they put the witches," he warned, "so you'd better watch out!"

"That's not where they put the witches," she corrected him with a toss of her head. "They got ducked in the ducking chair over there," pointing to an area next to the life-size replica of the ship *Deliverance*. "Do you know the story about this ship?"

Christopher shook his head.

"Sir George Somers and a party of colonists were on their way to Virginia when their vessel, the *Sea Venture*, hit a reef off the east coast of Bermuda in 1609. The colonists completed the journey by building a new ship, the *Deliverance*, out of the wreckage."

"Clever colonists!"

It had been a long day so they decided to make an early night of it. Back in front of Karyn's door at the Hilltop, Christopher gently kissed her good night, and they agreed to meet at eight the next morning in the breakfast room.

CHAPTER THREE

The sun was shining in through the open car windows, the wind gently lifting Karyn's silky hair. After meeting Christopher for breakfast earlier in the morning, she'd remembered the phone number Susan had given her of an acquaintance of hers who was a native Bermudian. Upon hearing they were in St. George, Vernon Jones had insisted on picking them up and taking them on a full-day's tour of his island. He arrived about half an hour later in a well-kept, white Ford. After the introductions were made, they were on their way.

Tourists were not allowed to rent cars in Bermuda, although taxicabs, mopeds, and bicycles were available for their use. Vernon pointed out that the number of cars in Bermuda was strictly regulated to one per household, and only residents were permitted to drive. He was soon chatting about his life and the history of the island.

"Bermuda's name comes from a Spaniard, Juan de Bermúdez, who discovered the island sometime in the early sixteenth-century."

"I thought Bermuda was a British colony," Karyn interjected in a puzzled voice.

"So it is. The oldest remaining colony. You see, the Spaniards didn't claim this land for their country. They were probably forced ashore by a storm and left again shortly thereafter. An English admiral, on his way to

Virginia, was shipwrecked here one hundred years later and claimed it for the Crown."

"Was that the same group that built the *Deliverance?*"

"That's correct. I suppose you've already seen the full-scale replica of the ship in St. George."

"Yes, we did," Christopher confirmed.

"Bermuda is a very friendly place," Vernon went on in his gentle English accent. "Everybody knows everyone else." As if to demonstrate that, he waved out the window at the doorman of the hotel they were passing.

"Hey, George, what's happening!"

Christopher turned to grin at Karyn; somehow that slang sounded strange after the preciseness of his British inflection. Vernon's first stop was the Castle Harbour Hotel, one of the older, more elegant hotels on the island. It had an unobstructed view of Castle Harbour with its brilliant, turquoise water. Karyn took several photographs, hoping that her camera would be able to capture the truly striking color of the shimmering water. The entire island seemed to be bathed with a bright white light that accentuated the palette of colors, the way a white mat accentuates a colorful painting.

"Can you see that island way in the distance?" Vernon asked, pointing to a long U-shaped island off the peninsula past Tucker's Town, a sanctuary for American, Canadian, and British millionaires. "That entire island belongs to one man. All that land for himself. He has his house there and his own beach."

As they continued on their way, they took a quick drive through Tucker's Town, with Vernon pointing out some of the more expensive houses and describing the occupants and their life-styles. Apparently, his wife had worked for most of these families at one time or another, before she took up the ministry. She was a very good cook, and her services had been much in demand.

Vernon stopped the car and showed them a lovely,

small garden that was surrounded by high walls and had a locked wrought-iron gate. He explained that the garden gate was locked because this was the only bit of American grass on the island, and people kept walking over it! The native grass was tough and looked a lot like clipped weeds. This garden was obviously well-tended; the grass looked as smooth as velvet.

The maze of narrow streets was traversed with stately ease, until Vernon pulled into a parking lot at the end of one of them. They got out and walked a short distance, against a fairly stiff breeze, stopping when they got to the edge of a bluff. Looking down Karyn saw the rock formation called Natural Arches, which was shaped by the sea washing out the center of the enormous rocks.

Grinning, Vernon commented, "This is a favorite place for honeymooners when the weather is a little warmer. They return to the States and say they made love under the Natural Arches."

Thinking of the gritty sand, Karyn imagined that it couldn't be that comfortable a location and decided she'd prefer a less exotic setting herself! As if reading her thoughts, Christopher grinned and leaned down to note, "I agree with you; too sandy!"

Karyn flashed him a startled look at the accuracy of his telepathy, then hurried up to where Vernon was waiting for them next to a large bush. Pulling off one of the leaves, he turned to hand it to Karyn. The leaf was about the size of both her hands put together.

"If you cover that leaf with glue, you will have a fan that will last you a lifetime!"

"Why thank you, Vernon. What kind of leaf is this?"

"It's a grape-tree leaf," he explained.

On their way across the bluff to the car Christopher murmured a humorous aside. "How are you going to get that past U.S. Customs, Mrs. Reid?"

Their return to the car prevented an answer on Karyn's

part. Since it was nearing lunchtime, they stopped in Paget Parish at a restaurant recommended by Vernon. It wasn't fancy, but it was definitely a popular spot, judging from the number of occupied tables. Karyn and Christopher both had the specialty of the house, scallops, while Vernon settled for a club sandwich. He also ordered a ginger beer.

"What's ginger beer?" Karyn inquired curiously.

"Actually, it's more a ginger pop than a beer," he defined. As the waitress brought his drink, he offered it to Karyn to taste, which she did.

"The soda in it makes it good for the digestion," he explained. Karyn nodded and handed his drink back to him. It tasted just as he'd described.

While they waited for their meal Vernon explained the geographical layout of Bermuda and where they had been so far. The islands were arranged in a fishhook shape, and Karyn discovered that there were nine parishes, or counties, in Bermuda. The town of St. George, on the northeastern tip of St. George's island was, naturally, in St. George's Parish. Moving in a westerly direction, the next parish was Hamilton, although the capital of Hamilton was not located in that parish! Tucker's Town and Grotto Bay were in Hamilton Parish, which is connected to St. George by a long causeway across Castle Harbour.

Next came Smith's Parish, where Vernon lived. Both Smith's Parish and neighboring Devonshire Parish consisted of rolling green countryside, reminding Karyn a bit of the pictures she'd seen of the English countryside. They'd even caught sight of some cows grazing in a field, and Vernon pointed out that several dairies were located in the area.

"We've been through five of the nine parishes," Vernon continued. "After lunch, we'll go into Hamilton, which is in Pembroke Parish. I'll show you around town and then you can stop and look at the shops for a bit. Afterward, we'll go down to the south shore to see all of our fabulous beaches in Warwick and Southampton Parishes."

The scallops were as good as Vernon had promised. Coated with lightly seasoned breadcrumbs, they melted in Karyn's mouth. She and Christopher both polished off their dishes, even though the helpings were by no means small. After lunch Vernon assisted them back into his car, and they headed toward Hamilton.

The speed limit throughout Bermuda was thirty-two kilometers, or twenty miles per hour, so they were able to enjoy the scenery at a leisurely pace. As they neared the capital, the traffic got noticeably heavier and Karyn was surprised to see several roundabouts used instead of corners to feed traffic into the city. They were informed that Hamilton was one of the world's smallest capital cities, with an area of only 180 acres.

Vernon drove past the central bus station, which Karyn recognized from the day she'd met Christopher on the boat. Was it only the day before yesterday? she thought to herself in amazement. She couldn't imagine living without him now. Those dark days after his disappearance were locked away in a distant compartment in her mind.

They continued on into the center of town. A large cruise ship was moored in the harbor, which was right alongside the main street. Christopher explained that usually such ships had to moor farther from land because the water wasn't deep enough closer in. Hamilton was the exception, which enabled Karyn to get her first close-up view of such a huge ship. It was several stories high and as long as two football fields! The dockside area was bustling with tourists who were departing and arriving to and from their floating hotel. Vernon pulled into a convenient parking place, and they agreed to meet him again in one hour.

Walking down the main shopping street, Front Street, Karyn despaired over only having one hour to shop in the large selection of beautiful stores, until Christopher, noticing her wistful expression, promised, "We'll come back later in the week and do some more in-depth looking around."

Her hand slid into his as she shot him a glowing smile in appreciation.

"There are so many shops to choose from, you almost don't know where to begin," she exclaimed.

"Let's start here," Christopher suggested, going inside a small mall of shops. The first one they entered happened to be a jewelry store. The three-figured price tags on the glittering objects in the display cases indicated that wealth was a requirement for prospective buyers.

On top of one of the cases was a selection of pastel shell chokers. Karyn stopped to admire one in light purple. A sales clerk appeared and inquired charmingly if she could be of assistance. Karyn asked the price and was pleasantly surprised to hear that it was less than ten dollars. The monetary system in Bermuda was based on the American dollar, which was generally accepted throughout the island.

Noting the unusual color, she inquired if the shells had been dyed. The clerk laughed and told her no; they were naturally that color. As Karyn prepared to pay for her purchase, Christopher covered her hand with his and spoke up.

"Please, allow me. I'd like to buy you a memento to remind you of this trip."

Tongue in cheek, Karyn responded, "I'll have you to remind me of this trip!"

"Oh, I'll be reminding you of a lot of things." His glinting blue eyes swept her body with a look that caused her heart to thump. "But I'd like to buy you something that will remind you just of Bermuda," he concluded. Christopher pocketed the small box the sales clerk had put the necklace in, and as they moved on, whispered in her ear. "I want to be able to put it on you myself and receive your personal thanks."

She felt the heat steal into her cheeks as she answered, "Aha, you have devious motives."

"You bet!"

They browsed through an array of stores full of luxury imports, from soft cashmere sweaters to delicate china and crystal. Karyn purchased a cedar box for her parents at one of the souvenir shops, and then it was time to meet Vernon again.

He was sitting in his car waiting for them, a group of men surrounding the open front door. Vernon introduced one of them as his brother-in-law who was in the water business. As they drove on, he explained that the only source of fresh water on the island was rainwater. The precious commodity was caught on terraced limestone roofs designed to collect and drain the water into underground storage tanks. It seemed that the distinctive island architecture was not only picturesque but also practical. On those occasions when this conservation system did not provide sufficient quantities, it became necessary to order water the way some people would order milk, and it would be delivered in a similar way. According to Vernon it was a profitable business.

Before leaving Hamilton, he drove them past the Sessions House, where the Supreme Court and the House of Assembly were located. Vernon pointed out that the Bermudian Parliament was the oldest in the British Commonwealth. His opinions of the current members of the Assembly were wrapped up in his description of them as "the forty thieves"! Politics were the same the world over, Karyn thought to herself with a grin.

The traffic thinned as they left Hamilton and took the turn onto South Road, which brought them close to the lovely world-famous beaches of the south shore. There were several pull-offs where Vernon stopped to allow them to take photographs of the wide expanses of storybook beaches that were gently caressed by the lapping aqua water.

At Horseshoe Bay, which takes its name from the curved shape of the beach, they stopped and got out to walk around. There weren't many bathers, for the breeze made swimming a little chilly. The curiously pink-tinged sand was powder-fine. Recalling the bottles of sand sold in the shops, Karyn took a little pillbox from her purse and poured a very small amount of sand into it for another memento of Bermuda. Looking closely at the sample she could see the minute pieces of pink coral that were the source of the beaches' unusual color.

Karyn sat down on the talc-soft sand to enjoy the picture-postcard view before her. Christopher and Vernon elected to climb one of the large hills along the beach to get an eagle-eye view. White-crested waves tumbled onto the beach with rhythmic regularity. A bird—perhaps a sandpiper—foraged for food along the water's edge. Grabbing her camera, she slowly followed it, her fingers poised on the shutter. The bird eventually paused and looked her way, but only after she'd stalked it all over the beach.

Putting her camera back in its case, she looked up at the hill to see how the men had progressed. Christopher waved down to her from his position at the top. Karyn made her way back across the beach to where she'd left their belongings and waited for the men to descend from the heights.

It was near evening when they made their final stop at Gibbs Lighthouse, the first cast-iron lighthouse in the world. They had passed some of the island's most exclusive hotels on their way around the south shore. Karyn's favorite was the hotel that was situated on its own island right off the coast. It was built in a U-shape, with the sea on one end and a private pool and dock area on the other.

She silently commended the ingenious architect who had designed it.

The road leading up to Gibbs Hill Lighthouse curved around the 245-foot hill on which it was located. They were the only visitors that late in the day. Laid out in front of them were a string of over two dozen islands nestled in Hamilton Harbour. Through the haze in the distance, you could just make out the buildings of Hamilton. Right off the shore in the Little Sound, they could see a collection of small islands, some of which were little more than protruding rocks. They stood and admired the beginning of the sunset as it spread its radiant colors across the sky.

"This is really beautiful," Karyn sighed in admiration.

Vernon nodded his agreement. "You should have seen it in 1976 when those tall ships were in the harbor." At Karyn's look of surprise he went on to explain. "The tall ships that went to New York for your bicentennial celebration started here. That is, they gathered here in order to make the run to New York in one large group. You know they came from all over the world. At night, the tiny lights strewn across their masts would cast sparkling reflections on the water. The morning they left, crowds of people converged along the entire coastline to see them sail out. I tell you, it was a sight I'll never forget!"

Karyn could well imagine the picture those tall-masted sailing ships had presented. She'd only seen them on television as they had sailed into New York on the fourth of July, but that sight had given her goose bumps and brought tears to her eyes. Needless to say, the ships had not come to Nebraska, where the nearest large body of water was Lake Michigan, over 500 miles away!

Tired, but well satisfied with their day, they made their way back to the car. Vernon drove them straight back to the Hilltop and made arrangements to pick them up the next morning for a small trip around St. George and St. David on this end of the island.

58

There was a little over an hour before dinner, so Karyn decided to wash her hair. She had just finished drying it with her hand-held, compact travel drier when there was a knock at her door.

"Who is it?"

"It's me, Christopher."

Tying the belt of her beige robe a little tighter around her slim waist, she opened the door to let him in.

"Can you help me with this damned cuff link; I can't get it done up!" he complained crossly.

She slid the offending cuff link into place with no trouble, admiring his handsome profile as she stepped back. He looked devastatingly attractive in dinner dress, the stark white shirt contrasting sharply with his dark tan.

"Thank you. I'm sorry to interrupt your preparations." Putting out his hand, he lifted a few strands of her still-damp hair. "You shouldn't be walking around with wet hair," he scolded her. "Here, give me the brush and I'll brush it dry for you."

He guided Karyn over to the corner of the bed, sat her down, then stood behind her and slowly ran the brush through her luxuriously thick hair. Karyn closed her eyes in appreciation; she had always enjoyed this, finding the stroking movements very relaxing. Christopher had carefully smoothed all the tangles out of her shining tresses when she heard him urgently whisper her name.

She trembled, her body mirroring the desire reflected in the cadence of his seductive voice. His hand drifted over her hair, then continued down her smooth shoulder to cherish the delicate curve of her breast. Dropping down next to her on the bed, his lips met hers in a slow, softly stimulating kiss that developed into a more passionate embrace as something deep within her responded to his magical touch. Her hands twined themselves around his neck and her body arched closer to his. The seductive movement caused the belt on her robe to loosen, revealing

59

more of her body to his caressing hands. His lips followed suit, leaving a fiery stream of kisses across her shoulder to the base of her throat, where he could feel the throbbing of her pulse. A moan of ecstasy passed her lips before his mouth reclaimed hers in an intoxicating exploration of her senses. Her body was fluid beneath his as her hands crept up his neck to comb through his tousled brown hair.

His lips left hers to tantalize the corners of her mouth and brush over her flushed cheeks and brilliant eyes. He teased her with a series of provocatively swift kisses that left her kindling emotions out of control until his lips caught hers and held them in a fervent caress that was almost an act of possession in itself. Her hands slid down his body, wanting to please him as much as he was pleasing her. His breath caught in his throat as she slowly undid the buttons of his shirt, one by one, and wrapped her arms around his muscular back. Now there was nothing between his firm supple body and hers. His body began trembling when he felt her breasts swell against him as she wriggled closer.

Karyn felt on fire with turbulent desires she'd never experienced before. Kissing him wasn't enough; she wanted to be part of him. Christopher obviously felt the same, and her emotions spiraled as he began an erotic exploration of the pleasure points of her body, caressing them first with his sensitive hands and then his warm mouth.

"Oh, honey, you're beautiful!" he gasped hoarsely, his voice aching with unfulfilled needs. His vivid blue eyes flared with ravenous hunger as he eagerly urged her to caress him in return. Her hands tentatively slid down his back, slowly touching each vertebra in his spine, her fingers inching over his skin as if trying to memorize the very feel of him. He nibbled on her earlobe, inhaling her fresh fragrance. Gaining confidence, she moved her hands around the curve of his waist, glorying at the feel of his hard rib cage through the tanned virility of his skin.

When she felt his caresses lower to her soft stomach and below, Karyn caught his wandering hand and held it, as fear brought reality flooding back to her. She realized that they were both lying on her small single bed, bodies merged from nape to hip. The pounding in her breast was not from her heart, as she'd thought, but from his, for nothing separated them from the waist up. The belt of her robe had come loose during their embrace, and while the material still covered her arms and legs, it had gapped alarmingly to reveal all the curves above her waist. Trepidation flickered through her as in one fluid movement, Christopher rose from the bed, taking her with him to drop down into a nearby chair, where he enfolded her in his arms.

They were both shuddering from the impact of their released emotions. His unsteady fingers closed the gaping robe, his knuckles brushing her chin as he held the material together.

"It's all right," he reassured her huskily. "I'm under control. But my God, you're a seductress! When, Karyn, when? When will you be ready for us to be husband and wife in every sense of the word? I know I promised not to rush you and I won't. I just want to know how you feel. There are things we'd have to prepare for first."

"Like what?" she questioned, her voice sounding unnatural to her.

"Well, I, for one, would like a double bed. The single beds are so small I'm afraid we won't be able to really enjoy ourselves for fear of falling off!"

She smiled, her emotions settling down to a more normal rate as his voice calmed her.

"Do you feel like picking the day for the great event? Look at it as if you were choosing the day of our wedding, because that day will be our true merging."

Gazing into his indigo eyes, Karyn appreciated the truth of his words. After the past hour there was no way she could kid herself that they would be able to control their desires much longer. They had been through so much—it seemed a shame to waste their time together by putting limitations on it. Surely, once she was his in every way, her foolish fears of his deserting her would disappear. Having made this decision she shakily promised him, "To-morrow."

"Are you sure?"

She nodded her assent.

"I love you. Do you believe me?" he asked, as if sensing her uncertainty.

"Oh, yes," she answered fervently. Held close to him like this, she did believe he loved her, as she loved him with all her heart. It was only when she was apart from him that the doubts crept in.

Deciding not to test their control any further, Karyn brushed her lips against his before getting up to get dressed. She pulled the closet door open and grabbed the first dress she laid her eyes on. It happened to be a teal-blue slip-dress with black polka dots. Taking it into the bathroom she locked the door and swiftly changed, smoothing the thin straps that held up the top before clasping a wide, black, elastic belt around her waist.

Christopher was reading some of the tourist bureau information when she entered the room. He looked up, his lips forming a silent whistle of appreciation, while his eyes seemed to stroke her body as they warmly appraised her.

With trembling hands she quickly applied a light touch of eye shadow and slid into her black, high-heeled sandals. When she went to apply lipstick, his voice stopped her.

"You don't need it. Your lips seem to be naturally red as it is!" he softly taunted her. "Your cheeks, too!" he noted as she blushed from his observations.

Pirouetting lightly in front of him, she pertly asked, "Will I pass?"

"Oh, you'll pass. In fact, I'm not sure it's safe to let you out looking so good. But then I know it's not safe to stay here with you, so get thee behind me, Satan!" he groaned. "We're off to dinner."

Christopher gallantly opened the door for her, and they set off at a leisurely rate toward the restaurant.

"Do you know what American tourists are called in Bermuda?"

"Is it repeatable?" Karyn questioned, knowing that Americans were often unpopular abroad.

"Certainly! I'm not about to launch into any off-color humor," he protested. "They're called longtails."

"Longtails?"

"The national bird of Bermuda, a type of sea gull," he explained.

"How did we get a name like that?"

"Because the longtails migrate to the island when the weather gets warmer for summer, the way the tourists do, always returning to the same point. They leave for warmer climates in the fall."

"How do you know that?"

"I've got my sources," he said airily.

They had an enjoyable dinner. During the meal Christopher informed her that he had reservations at the nightclub in the large hotel nearby.

"They've got a very popular steel band scheduled and I thought you might like to hear them."

"Why didn't you mention it earlier?" she protested. "I might not have been wearing something suitable for a nightclub."

"You put everything clean out of my mind earlier," he admitted, a smile tugging at his lips at the memory. "Except for one subject, and that had nothing to do with nightclubs! With entertainment maybe!" Satisfied that he'd stolen her composure, Christopher continued. "As to suitable attire I would say that you are wearing the perfect outfit for . . ." he paused meaningfully, watching her cheeks redden, ". . . spending the night on the town," he calmly finished.

They tried to get a taxi up to the hotel, but there was none to be found, so they simply took the shuttle bus up. Perhaps not so elegant, Karyn thought to herself with a grin, but certainly quicker than waiting over an hour for a cab.

The nightclub was on the tenth floor of the hotel. It was very crowded, and even with reservations, they still had to share a table with another couple. As it turned out, the other couple were the manager of the steel band and his wife. Several members of the band stopped at the table before their act. A typical pop group was currently on the small stage, blaring out the standard numbers.

"Would you like to dance?" Christopher asked her.

She hesitated. "Maybe later."

He heaved a sigh of relief. "Thank goodness! You know, you could probably faint in that crowd, and no one would know it because the sheer mass of humanity would prop you up. I was willing to risk my limbs for you, but I'm glad I won't have to."

The pop group wound up their last song and left the stage. The manager, Graham, went to organize the setting up of the steel drums. Graham's wife, Ginger, was a former model from New York.

"We've moved to Bermuda now, and we're shocked at the cost of living here! New York City is not a cheap place, by any means, but to pay over two dollars for a quart of orange juice!" She shook her head. "I guess it's because everything has to be brought in—Bermuda being an island and all."

Karyn nodded. Any response she might have made was curtailed as the lights dimmed in preparation for the steel band's appearance. She jumped at the thundering volume of the first song's opening bars, not being prepared for the decibel level of the music. At first, she'd suspected that the

64

sound system was turned too high, but then Ginger leaned across the table, yelling to make herself heard above the music.

"They're good, aren't they? And this is without any kind of amplification. The instruments are this loud all by themselves!"

Karyn's eardrums gradually became accustomed to the surge of sound, and she began to enjoy the music. There were six members in the band. One of them was a vocalist and another was a drummer. A third played the congas and other small percussion instruments. The remaining three were playing the steel drums, two tenor pans, and one bass pan. After their first song the vocalist briefly described the history of steel bands. After World War II the Allies' refueling gasoline drums had been left behind. The islanders tried hitting them and enjoyed the sounds that could be obtained. It had now been lifted to an art, with an entire range of sounds available.

She enjoyed their rendition of the "William Tell Overture" the most. The audience must've agreed with her, for they gave the band a standing ovation. Their encore was "Rhapsody in Blue."

After the performance the pop band reclaimed the stage. A number of the patrons began drifting out, so Karyn and Christopher were able to take to the dance floor without threat of bodily harm. Wrapped in her husband's arms she felt lighter than air. Her hand rested against the lapel of his jacket, dreamily fingering the smooth material. They slowly drifted across the room until the music quickened to a disco beat. Back at their table Karyn couldn't contain a yawn, even though she tried to.

"Caught you. Straight home and bed for you," he diagnosed. "Alone for the moment," he added wickedly, "you're going to need your rest!"

65

Outside her room Christopher lightly brushed his thumb across her parted lips.

"I think I've had enough stimulation for one day, so I won't kiss you good night. I'll see you in the morning," and with a smoldering look, he was gone.

CHAPTER FOUR

Sunday dawned bright and sunny. This was the day she was going to love Christopher, and he was going to love her, completely. Karyn ignored the slight apprehension she felt at that thought and concentrated on their future together.

She got so wrapped up in her daydreaming that she nearly missed breakfast and found she had to rush to get ready in time. Remembering that they planned on stopping at a beach later in the afternoon, Karyn pulled her swimsuit on underneath her outfit. The white canvas trousers and short-sleeve blue cotton shirt printed with white flowers looked casually elegant. A white belt over the shirt completed the ensemble.

Christopher was already seated at the breakfast table with a cup of coffee in front of him. He rose as she walked in and smiled at her. There were only two other people still in the dining room, an elderly couple from New Jersey who had arrived yesterday by yacht. Breathless from her run up the stairs, she apologized for being late.

Vernon met them as prearranged. The day was blustery with a few clouds scuttling across the sky. Vernon drove them first to Fort St. Catherine, where replicas of the British Crown Jewels are kept, and then to reconstructed Gates Fort. He guided them over to the edge of the water, overlooking a narrow channel of bay.

"This is known as the Cut," he explained. "Its full name

67

is Town Cut, and this is where all the ships, including cruise ships, have to pass to get to St. George's Island." Vernon pointed out the buoys on both sides of the relatively narrow channel that indicated the safe path the ships should follow. As they stood there, a good-sized sailing yacht came from St. George, went through the Cut and out into the open sea.

Making their way back to the car, Vernon continued his narrative. "This fort was built to keep away the Spanish ships. In all, only two shots were ever fired from both of these forts."

"Apparently that was sufficient to scare the Spanish away!" Christopher laughed.

They had to drive through St. George in order to reach St. David, an island right across St. George's Harbour where the Civil Air Terminal and the U.S. Naval Air Station were both located.

"The people of St. David's stay together and don't mix with the rest of us," they were informed. "Until the war, that is. Then the Americans came and built this airstrip out into Castle Harbour. That's what really brought in the tourists, because after the war we converted part of the strip the Americans had built into our own Civil Airport. We now have 747's landing from Europe several times a week, as well as daily flights from the States."

As they went past the air base, the scenery became more rugged. There were no large towns or cities on St. David. They stopped at St. David's Head and got out to take a look around, discovering an old World War I fortress that had been built as a lookout for U-boats. They climbed up over the ruins to the top of the cliffs. The wind was straight off the Atlantic now and was very stiff. Karyn appreciated Christopher's strong arm around her for both warmth and protection.

"This is the first land this wind has hit since Spain," he informed her, "and that's over 3500 miles away!"

She supposed that explained why the wind was so fierce. They turned to see Vernon waving his hands in excitement, indicating that they should join him. They did so and he pointed out their first sighting of a group of longtails. The birds made their nests in the high cliffs so they wouldn't be disturbed. Karyn thought they chose well; she couldn't see anyone but a nut climbing those sheer cliffs just to see a bird's nest!

From her first glance she was able to appreciate how these graceful birds gained their name of longtails. Unlike other sea gulls, they had long, white tails measuring over six inches, which stood out behind them when they glided in the wind. As they turned to and fro, she was able to see the black-tipped wings silhouetted against the sky.

St. David was much wilder than the rest of Bermuda, its rugged cliffs and coastline reminding Karyn of a recent television series that was set in Cornwall, England. Deciding that the wind was too brisk on this end of the island, they headed for a sheltered beach along the north shore, John Smith's Beach. Vernon explained that the south shore beaches would be exposed to the prevailing winds.

He dropped them off at the beach and arranged to pick them up at the end of the afternoon. An uncrowded stretch of coralline sand beckoned invitingly. Initially the water was rather cold due to the difference in air and water temperatures. The intermittent sunshine was combed by soft sea breezes. Karyn had never swum in salt water before and was surprised at the buoyancy it provided. They frolicked in the sea for some time before she returned to their towels, tired after their horseplay. She spread herself on the warm surface and enjoyed the feel of the sun soaking into her skin. A few clouds scurried across the sky, their shadows following suit on the sand. The beach was much quieter than the pool had been a few days ago, and Karyn fell asleep.

When she awoke, she noticed that the sun was hidden

behind clouds and that she felt chilly. Christopher was stretched out beside her, reading a thriller. Looking at her watch, she realized that she'd been asleep for nearly two hours!

She got up and walked down to the water's edge, but couldn't raise any enthusiasm to do more than paddle in the waves with her feet. The beach was practically deserted now, Karyn observed, absently scratching her arm. In doing so she noticed that her skin felt sensitive to the touch and recalled in dismay that she hadn't applied her sunscreen as she had meant to after lying down.

Returning to Christopher, she spread some cream on her back, feeling rather like the farmer who bolted the barn door after the horse had run out. He noticed her frown and bent over to ask what the problem was. When she explained, he became concerned and took the cream from her to lightly smooth it on her back, carefully making sure that he didn't miss any areas.

"You're going to have one hell of a burn. I should have watched you more closely," he castigated himself.

"And I should have known better," she responded wryly.

Luckily, Vernon was early, and they were able to return to their guesthouse sooner than anticipated. Her back was not really painful yet, so after changing into a long-sleeve sheer cotton shirt in lemon-yellow and a matching cotton skirt, Karyn insisted that they make their way back into St. George and stop at a little tea room for English high tea. Christopher had been at Oxford University before coming to the University of Nebraska, and she wondered if the meal brought back any memories for him, or if he had never forgotten that period in his life.

When they returned to their rooms, Karyn knew that she was in for a restless night. She made her excuses to Christopher and decided to make an early night of it, carefully stretching out on the bed trying to read. Her back was much too painful to lie on, so she was forced to rest on her side. When Christopher came to inquire about her a short while later, she told him she didn't think she was in the mood for any dinner. He didn't press her, and after making sure there was nothing she needed, left to eat dinner on his own. Almost two hours later, she was surprised to hear a gentle knocking on her door.

"It's me, Christopher."

Karyn got up, but had to stand beside the bed for a moment because the room began to spin around like a merry-go-round at a carnival. She gingerly made her way to the door and let him in, then clasped her hand to her mouth as it suddenly occurred to her that this was the night she'd promised to become his wife.

"Christopher, I'm sorry. I really don't feel very well. I think we're going to have to postpone our . . . ummmm . . . arrangement until later," she said unsteadily. Seeing the way his expression hardened, she whispered, "I really am very sorry."

His face was expressionless now as he gently assisted her back to bed, where she lay shivering. The room temperature felt cool against her hot skin.

"I stopped at a pharmacist before going to dinner and he gave me a few antihistamines for you. You've got an allergic reaction to overexposure to the sun, which this medication should help alleviate," he explained, pouring her a drink of water from the Thermos on the nightstand next to her bed. She took the pill from his hand and swallowed it with the water.

Karyn drifted in and out of sleep throughout the night. Nothing was very clear to her except for Christopher's reassuring presence as he periodically got her a cool drink or soothed her fevered brow. She had no recollection of crying out, "Christopher, where are you? Don't leave me!"

A spasm of pain crossed his handsome face as he realized how difficult the past year had been for her. The

71

strain of his amnesia had never been harder to handle than it was that night. Shadows of the past flitted across the walls of his memory, but despite all his attempts to pin them down, they remained elusively out of reach. Discouraged, he came back to the present.

How could Karyn have suspected him of wanting to consummate their marriage when she was so ill? Only an insensitive brute would've considered it under the circumstances. Yet he knew he couldn't be angry with her—she had suffered enough pain on his account. His fist clenched in impotent rage at the impenetrable screen obstructing his memory.

The sky was just beginning to lighten when she awoke feeling tired but much better. Turning her head on the pillow, she saw her husband slumped in a chair that he had pulled up next to her bed. Her face softened with love as she realized that he had spent the entire night at her side. Putting out her hand, she tenderly touched his arm. He immediately leaned forward and asked, "How are you feeling? Do you want anything?"

"I'm feeling much better, really." He sighed in relief. "But there is something I would like."

"What?"

"I would like you to go to bed and get some rest yourself. That chair doesn't look very comfortable." He still hesitated so she went on to reassure him. "I really am much better. I'll just take things easy this morning and stay out of the sun. The pills have taken the worst reactions away. Please get some rest."

Christopher reluctantly complied, promising to return in three hours. By then Karyn was up and dressed, feeling much more like herself. Her back was still painful to the touch, and she wasn't able to wear a bra because the fastening proved too much against her tender, red skin. Instead, she wore a loose aqua rayon shirt with her white trousers. She had a sun hat and sunglasses close at hand for sitting on the veranda at the front of the house. Karyn ate a light breakfast, just toast and coffee. The other guests showed their concern by inquiring about how she felt.

As she settled into a comfortable deck chair on the shaded veranda, she realized that she and Christopher might as well take this opportunity to discuss the future. They had already discussed their past and the present, but the details of what would happen after Bermuda were still up in the air.

The guesthouse was quiet, all the guests having departed to complete assorted itineraries of sightseeing. Karyn slid the sunglasses on to shield her eyes from the glare of the sun. Even though she was sitting in the shade, the extraordinary light that bathed the island seemed to reflect from everything it touched.

Christopher joined her, worriedly questioning her. "Are you sure you're feeling better? You wouldn't like to lie down again?"

"I'm fine," she assured him.

She waited until he'd settled into the chair next to her before beginning.

"Christopher, we haven't really talked about the practical matters concerning our future."

"Like 'do you have enough money to support a wife?' for example," he lightly quipped.

"Well, do you?"

Christopher looked a little taken aback at her directness. "Yes, I do have enough money to support both of us."

Karyn had to laugh at his wary expression. "I'm really not after your millions. But a lot has happened in the year we've been apart. I'm not at all familiar with your current life. All I know is that you're living in Chicago and that you're in charge of a computer consulting firm that your uncle left you. That's it!"

"I didn't realize that I hadn't told you more. First I

73

forgot to remember you, and now I forget I ever forgot you," he berated himself. "I'm sorry, what do you want to know? Never mind, dumb question. The answer is everything, right?" Christopher turned to her for confirmation, which he received by her quick nod.

"I suppose I'll begin with where I live. I've got a house I bought shortly after I moved to Chicago. It's a two-bedroom, contemporary-style A-frame located in the western suburbs. I usually take the commuter train in to work unless I have to stop to see a client, in which case I drive."

"What kind of car?"

He named an expensive German import.

"Color?"

"Silver."

"Very distinguished-sounding," she decided with a grin.

"You should see the way it handles," he enthused. "I've driven it on some of the most slippery roads in the country and in some of the worst weather conditions imaginable. It handles like a dream. Front wheel drive, rack and pinion steering . . ."

Karyn's cough interrupted him. "Could we get back to the matter at hand?"

"I suppose I was getting a little off the beaten track there, but you did ask. To continue, the house is not terribly large; however, it suits my needs. The kitchen has a dishwasher and the other necessary appliances. Let's see . . . what else is there?" He paused a moment to consider.

"What are you going to tell people when you get back?" Karyn interjected.

"Tell people?"

"Am I right in presuming that none of your friends or acquaintances know you're married?"

"Oh, I see."

"The other thing is . . ." she nervously paused to look

down at her clenched hands, "that is . . . you haven't actually asked me to come live with you yet," she finally blurted out.

"My God, you're absolutely right! I'm really not doing this properly at all, am I?"

He gracefully got up, only to drop to his knees next to her chair, where he took her hand and raised it to his lips.

"On bended knee I'm imploring you to come be my wife in the wilds of Chicago's western suburbs. Will you agree?"

"It sounds quite improper," she informed him, trying to contain her mirthful delight.

"Oh, it will be!" Christopher assured her with a meaningful glint in his deep blue eyes while his tongue caressed the sensitive skin between her fingers. She refused to drop her eyes, but could not control the excitement that heated her face.

"In that case, I accept!"

"Good." Dropping her hand, he calmly returned to his own chair.

Karyn flung him a slightly resentful look that made him grin. "I'll show my proper, and improper, appreciation when you've recovered from that sunburn and when we're alone." His voice held a wealth of promise.

"You do realize that I'll have to go back to Seattle, don't you?" she asked a few minutes later, returning to their original topic of discussion.

"No, I didn't," he denied. "Why?"

"For a number of reasons. First, all my belongings are there, and I can't ask Susan to pack them for me. I also have a job waiting for me, so I would have to give my employer official notice. Then there are the necessary arrangements to make, things I'll have to clear up. After all, meeting you like this was unexpected."

"You can phone your employer and explain the situation; I'm sure he'd understand. And Susan, if she's a friend of yours, won't mind packing your belongings and shipping them out. I'll hire a moving company to collect your furniture," he continued enthusiastically.

"Susan may not mind, but I would," Karyn protested. "And I don't have any furniture. That is, the furniture I have is stored in Lincoln. Oh no, I completely forgot about my parents!" she gulped, putting her hand to her mouth in consternation.

"What about them?"

"I'll have to tell them about us."

"Oh, I see," he nodded knowingly. "I don't suppose they've been thinking very highly of me this past year—the rake who married their daughter and then deserted her the same day. As I recall, your mother didn't really care for me to begin with, and all I'd done then was propose to you."

"They know how upset I've been this past year. They've got to realize how much you mean to me and how happy I must be now that we're together again. But I don't think I'll call them until I get back to Seattle. They'll understand." Karyn added "I hope" under her breath.

"Let's get back to this business about flying all the way to Seattle," he insisted. "It's miles past Chicago. You'd save money just getting off there and arranging the rest by phone."

"Darling, you've been very understanding these past few days," she said quietly. "Please understand that I have to do this for my own peace of mind. In my place I really think you'd be doing the same thing."

Christopher was silent for some time as he digested her statement.

"How long would it take?" he finally asked.

"I should be able to arrange everything in two-weeks time, if nothing unexpected happens."

"Like what?" he questioned sharply.

"If I knew that, it wouldn't be unexpected, would it?"

she gently chided. "Two weeks and then I'll be able to bring my things with me to move in with you."

"If it's really something you feel you have to do, then I guess I go along with it," he reluctantly allowed.

"So the plan is for me to use my ticket to return to Seattle and give notice to my employer and Susan as soon as I arrive. I settle all my affairs and pack my things to come join you. There may be some extra baggage," she worried. "I have several extra suitcases, but I believe you're only allowed two cases to check through. I'll have to make a note to check with the airlines."

"How are you flying to Seattle and when?"

"There is no direct flight; I change planes in Chicago."

"When?" he repeated.

"Let's see . . . this is Monday; my flight is on Saturday. What about you?" she exclaimed, suddenly realizing that she had no idea when he was scheduled to return. "I never thought . . ."

"Now you know how I feel," he grinned at her. "My reservation is for this Thursday, but I'll call the airlines right now to see if they can change it."

While he went indoors to make his phone call, Karyn tried to think of a suitable explanation for her parents. She didn't suppose she'd have much trouble with her father; however, her mother was another story. Christopher was right—she'd never really approved of him. He'd been much too worldly for her, having just come to Nebraska after three years at Oxford University. Karyn could still hear her mother's voice criticizing.

"American universities weren't good enough for him, humph!" she'd snorted in disgust. "What about all those Ivy League schools in the East? He is from Rhode Island, isn't he?" she demanded.

"Yes, he grew up in Rhode Island."

"I'm not even sure exactly where that is. Somewhere along the East Coast isn't it, along with all those fancy schools? But, oh no, he has to go off to England to get an education. Can you prove he really grew up in Rhode Island?"

"Why would I want to do that?" Karyn patiently asked.

"Because he could be anybody. He may have made this whole story up just to sound exotic. I've read of cases like that in the newspaper."

"Mother, really! You can tell by just talking to him that there is nothing deceitful or underhanded about Christopher. You can't really suspect him of something like that."

"Maybe not," her mother conceded. "But I do think you should wait."

"We're not exactly eloping. We set the date for May, that's five months away."

"I won't say any more," she sniffed. "I suppose it's your decision."

Karyn's thoughts were snatched back to the present by Christopher's return.

"What did they say?" she asked anxiously.

"What they usually say. They'll check into it and get back to me. The clerk didn't seem to think there would be a problem changing the reservation."

"Have you decided what you're going to tell your friends about us?"

"Well, I haven't actually been in Chicago long enough to form many close relationships. I am friendly on a casual basis with Bob Martin; he advises me on legal matters. I have filled him in briefly about my amnesia, but the people I work with don't know anything about it. I was able to survive on a day-to-day basis, and frankly, it is a little embarrassing to tell people about it. They tend to look at you as if you were crazy and might come at them with an ax or something. Since I was someone new coming in, they were already suspicious of me."

"How many people work for you?"

"There are about fifteen presently in the firm. I'm hoping to expand it to twenty within the next few months."

Karyn was impressed.

"Actually, my private life is no one's business but my own, and yours," he added with a warm smile that lit her heart. "What are your feelings about telling them that we met again in Bermuda and that now we're married? It's not a lie—it's just not a full explanation. And it would certainly simplify matters."

"What about Stella Dukane? Do you still keep in touch with her?"

"Yes, she's been most helpful in getting me settled in Chicago. She came down for a few weekends when I first moved into the house to help out. I'm hoping she and Bob Martin will make a go of things. I think there's something going on between them."

"Is she still in Milwaukee?"

"Now that you mention it, she is thinking of moving to Chicago. There are more job opportunities there because it's a larger city. Personally, I think that may just be an excuse," he confided.

"Excuse?" Karyn questioned sharply, extremely suspicious of this woman who had knowingly led Christopher astray by telling him he lived in Milwaukee.

"I think she really wants to be closer to Bob."

"Oh." For some reason instinct led Karyn to doubt that. She believed that Stella's reason was indeed an excuse, but she suspected that the truth was a desire to get closer to Christopher, not Bob Martin.

"She'll really be surprised to hear about you," he continued.

I bet she will, Karyn thought to herself!

"I also asked the airlines to make a reservation for your flight from Seattle to Chicago on the 29th—that's exactly two weeks after you get there. I'll take care of that. The ticket should be waiting for us at the airport on Saturday."

79

Mrs. Robertson's voice calling him to the telephone interrupted their discussion. He returned shortly with the news that his reservation had been changed and confirmed for Saturday.

"That's all settled then. I'll fly to Chicago on the 29th, and you'll tell everyone that you've gotten married in Bermuda. What about a wedding ring?" she questioned. "I've still got mine, but yours was lost in the accident." Another incident Karyn found more than a little suspicious. She couldn't help wondering if Stella had had something to do with it. "Shall we go into Hamilton this afternoon and look for another one?"

"Don't you want to take it easy today?" he asked her. "After all, you are still burned."

"I'm feeling much better, and by the looks of the weather, the sun isn't going to be much of a threat for a while," pointing to the layer of thick clouds that had blown in from the south. "It looks as though we're going to get some of that badly needed rain."

"That's right. Vernon did say that the water supply was getting rather low because it's been a very dry spring. All right, fate seems to decree that we go to Hamilton this afternoon, and who am I to fight that?"

"We'll just follow Bermuda's official motto."

"Which is?"

"Whither the fates lead us!"

Enjoying a casual dinner in an old-fashioned, English-style pub later that evening, Karyn paused to admire the new wedding band on her husband's left hand. It had taken a while, but they were finally able to find a plain, wide gold band, neither of them caring for anything fancy or gaudy.

"How's it feel to be a marked man?" she teased him.

Christopher's handsome face paled alarmingly.

"What is it?" Karyn asked in concern.

He put his hand to his forehead, as if to rub out a sudden

twinge of pain. His blue eyes were marked by hauntingly elusive memories.

"I thought I remembered something, something important," he muttered. "It's passed now."

"Does this happen often?" she questioned, regarding him with worried eyes.

He gave her a noncommittal answer and hurriedly changed the subject. On the surface Christopher had regained his urbane charm, yet all the while she sensed an underlying tension in him. It wasn't something she could put her finger on, so she chastised her fertile imagination and gave herself up to the pleasure of his company.

Their ensuing conversation ranged over a wide variety of topics from philosophy to politics. They were deep in a discussion about their favorite artists when they were interrupted by the waiter with the check. Glancing down at her watch, Karyn was shocked to see that they had been talking for three hours. It hadn't seemed like a quarter of that. The best way to kill time may be to work it to death, she considered with a smile, but the best way to enjoy time was to spend it with the one you loved.

It was quite late when they got back to the Hilltop and Karyn felt happy but exhausted. Her lids were drooping as she gave Christopher a drowsy good-night kiss. He laughingly bestowed a gentle peck on her forehead and ordered her to go straight to bed.

CHAPTER FIVE

Looking out from her window the next morning, Karyn was pleased to see the sun shining from a cloudless, blue sky. The air was fresh, filled with the scent of newly washed flowers. Although she could appreciate the islanders' need for fresh water, she was glad that the rain had ceased during the night so that today's activities need not be curtailed due to the weather.

Wearing beige cotton slacks and an oatmeal knit top, she walked into the breakfast room. It was early, so Christopher wasn't there yet. She took the opportunity to speak privately to Mrs. Robertson about the chance of trading their two single rooms for a double. The request made Karyn feel obligated to supply an explanation. She did so by saying that she and her husband had been separated and had a reconciliation in the romantic atmosphere of Bermuda. Mrs. Robertson was pleased that her country had instigated such a happy reunion and said she would have a double room available for them the following day.

Flushed with her success, Karyn walked back into the breakfast room with a smile on her lovely face, to find Christopher preparing to sit down at the table.

"You're looking like the proverbial Cheshire cat this morning. What gives?" he demanded.

"Mrs. Robertson informed me that a double room will be available for our use tomorrow," she told him quietly.

His expression matched hers as a smile lit his features.

The entrance of other guests prevented them from further discussion. It wasn't until breakfast was served that Karyn spoke again, and then it was to inquire about the day's agenda.

"I thought we'd go investigate the Bailey's Bay area. We could see the dolphin show: there's one scheduled every hour from 11:00 A.M. on. The Crystal Caves are nearby, and there are a lot of other sights to see in the general vicinity."

"Sounds good," Karyn agreed.

They took the bus to Bailey's Bay, having much less trouble than they did getting to the Botanical Gardens several days before, and got off at the stop just past the Causeway from St. George. They walked down the long drive leading to the Blue Grotto Dolphin Show, enjoying the beautiful weather, the colorful shrubs and flowers that edged the road along the way, and the sheer pleasure of being together in such glorious surroundings.

The dolphin show was held in a small cove at the end of the road. Several rows of boards had been set up for seating. As they made their way to a seat, Karyn was surprised to see a couple of cats wandering around the side of the grotto. Their presence was explained later when the show started and fresh fish were used as rewards for the dolphins. The trainer ended up throwing several of the fish to the cats, just to keep them out of his way.

It was an entertaining show, with several dolphins performing an assortment of tricks, including jumping over rods and through hoops. The highlight of the show was a fifty-foot jump by the dolphins to take fresh fish out of the trainer's hand. It started with first one, then two, and ended with all three dolphins jumping simultaneously while the trainer held fish in both hands and his mouth.

"I suppose you could be in danger of getting your teeth knocked out if you weren't careful," Christopher commented wryly. "I hope he has good dental coverage!"

After the show they strolled back down the long drive to the main road. They stopped at a pottery factory and looked around at the workshop, but Karyn didn't see anything she wanted to purchase so they moved on. The next stop was the ice cream parlor and there she did find something she wanted to buy. She had a scoop of fresh pistachio ice cream while Christopher chose banana and raisin. Taking their cones out to the terrace they sat down and enjoyed their treat.

"Here," Karyn held out her cone. "You've got to taste this."

Christopher obligingly licked the proffered cone and in turn offered her his for a taste.

"Ummm, that was good," she said as she licked the last remains of ice cream from her lips. "Now we'll have to do something to burn all those calories off!"

The Crystal Caves fit the bill perfectly. Guided tours of the caves were offered every hour. One was just leaving when they arrived, so Karyn and Christopher joined the tail end.

"The caves were discovered in 1907 when two young boys were playing ball, and the ball disappeared into a hole in the ground," their guide informed them.

As they followed the sloping path that led them down toward the bottom, Karyn thought that if she had been playing ball all those years ago, she would have left it in the hole, rather than coming down here, alone, after it. As the atmosphere got danker and more eerie, she grabbed hold of Christopher's hand. He squeezed her fingers reassuringly.

"They should put up a sign at the entrance stating that this trip could be dangerous to the emotional health of people suffering from claustrophobia." she decided.

"Do you?" he asked in sudden concern, not remembering.

"No, I don't. If I did, I'd have been long gone by now. It is a little creepy though," she shivered.

When they paused at the bottom, their guide told them that they were now 120 feet below the surface.

"See what I mean?" Karyn whispered.

The tour continued along a floating causeway that went through the caves. Thousands of stalactites and stalagmites were glistening in the man-made illumination, gleaming a pale white or green to form an unusual blend of colors. The guide stopped once again to say that with all the illumination you couldn't really get the true feeling of the cave. Then she threw a switch, and the lights all went out. There were several gasps from the group as they were thrown into total darkness, such as most of them had never experienced before.

Christopher decided to take this opportunity to give Karyn a reassuring kiss, but he found that his perceptions were affected by the inky blackness, and instead of kissing her lips as planned, he kissed her chin.

"Christopher, was that you?" she whispered.

"I should hope so!" he whispered back. "My aim was a little low. Sorry."

The guide switched the lights back on, to the relief of all, and they ended their tour by climbing the multitude of steps that brought them back to the surface.

"That certainly took care of all the calories from the ice cream, but now I'm starving." Christopher complained.

They stopped for lunch at an inn across from the ice cream parlor. The rest of the afternoon was spent visiting the other tourist spots, including the Perfume Factory and the Aquarium. As there was some distance between each attraction, Karyn's feet were aching by the end of the day.

She would have loved to soak in a hot tub, but they only had showers in their rooms, so she made do with that. Afterwards, she donned her full black-jersey skirt and added a purple silk blouse with a notched collar and three-quarter sleeves. She was pleased to see that her new purple shell necklace matched and was about to put it on when Christopher knocked on her door. The moment she let him in, he immediately spied the necklace hanging from her hand.

"You better not have been trying to wriggle out of our agreement," he warned.

"What?" she asked in total confusion.

"The agreement was that I would put the necklace on you myself and receive your personal thanks," repeating the words he had whispered in her ear after buying it for her in Hamilton.

He took the necklace from her unresisting fingers and gently turned her around.

"You could help matters by holding your hair out of the way," he suggested.

Karyn accommodatingly did so, leaving the vulnerable nape of her neck exposed to his wandering lips.

After a few moments, or were they only seconds, she gasped, "Christopher!"

"Ummmm?"

"What are you doing?"

"I'm getting the feel for my work," he muttered against her skin, his warm mouth provoking disconcerting quivers all along her nervous system.

Christopher stopped his stirring caress just in time, otherwise her knees may not have continued to support her. As it was, she felt like a mass of unset Jell-O. He fastened the necklace and slowly lowered her hair back over her shoulders.

Turning around, Karyn was informed, "Now it's your turn for your personal show of thanks."

Two can play at this game, she reflected, and decided to ruffle his composure the same way he had hers. She began her campaign by reaching up to brush her lips back and forth against his firm mouth, barely touching him.

86

When his lips began chasing hers, she quickly evaded him. Just when he thought he would have to raise his hands to hold her head still, her lips clung to his with a penetrating abandonment that made his senses swim and left them both shaken by the blazing eruption of thermal emotion.

Her actions had their desired effect as Christopher stepped back to wipe a shaking hand across his damp forehead. However, she hadn't reckoned on her own excitement, for the knowledge that she could excite him had in turn aroused her. They made a quick getaway from the intimate temptation of her bedroom, with Christopher reflecting her thoughts as he huskily murmured, "You did say the double room is available tomorrow, right?" His fervent "Thank God" in response to her nod was silently repeated by Karyn.

They had a fairly quiet dinner, the air filled with unfulfilled desires, while they both wished time would pass more quickly. Her feet were still aching, so they didn't take their normal after-dinner stroll. They sat out on a bench along the waterfront instead, enjoying the view.

He noticed Karyn surreptitiously removing her sandals to rub her feet.

"Sore feet? he asked sympathetically.

"It was rather a long walk today. The guidebooks don't tell you that all those listed attractions aren't right next to each other, as implied."

The next thing she knew, Christopher had swiftly reached down and put his strong fingers around her slender ankles, pulling her feet onto his lap, where he began to slowly massage them. The soothing movements of his fingers eased the ache in her feet, but started another ache in her heart.

She loved him so much. Was it wrong of her to be so forgiving, or so naïve as to believe his story on his say-so alone? Was she leaving herself wide open for more heartbreak by letting him walk back into her life after a year's absence and pick up where they had left off? These questions and others like them haunted her with cruel persistence. Her heart told her that she was right in following it, but her head kept niggling her with foreboding anxieties. Staring at his profile while he concentrated on relieving her pain, she temporarily ended her soul-searching with the conviction that Christopher was the kind of man a woman could feel safe with. He would never deliberately set out to hurt anyone.

"Better?" he asked her.

"Yes, much better," she answered both him and herself.

As the night air got cooler, they got up and went back to the Hilltop. Christopher dropped his coat around her shoulders to protect her from the chilled air. Outside her door they made their last evening farewells, because on the morrow they would be sharing the same room. Holding the lapels of his coat, he pulled her close to share a heady, magnetically stimulating kiss. His coat dropped from her shoulders as her arms rose to clasp themselves around his neck, fingers curling in his dark hair. Her receptive response inflamed his senses and he molded her curvaceous body more closely to his. His hands were beginning a thrilling exploration of the hidden softness under her blouse, when she pulled away, breathless.

"Good night," she whispered and fled to her room, knowing that if she hadn't left immediately, they would now be sharing her small, narrow single bed without waiting until tomorrow!

By early the next morning Karyn had most of her things packed in preparation for their move later that day. She only left out the red-checked long-sleeve shirt and black jeans that she planned on wearing. Feeling a slight nip in the air blowing through an open window, she decided to return and pull out a black sweater from her suitcase. Christopher was waiting for her at the top of the stairs leading to the breakfast room.

Dressed in beige cords that accentuated the whipcord strength of his long legs, he looked compellingly attractive. The sleeves of his black long-sleeve pullover sweater were pushed up to reveal his tanned forearms. The crisp white collar of his shirt, visible through the V neck of his sweater, framed the strong column of his throat. His brown hair was slightly ruffled, as if he had hurriedly tugged on the sweater at the last minute and hadn't stopped to comb it again afterwards.

They sat down at a table for four, joining a couple from Ireland who had recently immigrated to Canada. An enjoyable discussion concerning the differences between the Old World and the New accompanied their leisurely breakfast. Conflicting thoughts were exchanged on the adjustments necessary for a happy settlement in the new country.

Afterward, Mrs. Robertson discreetly pulled Karyn and Christopher aside to tell them their room was available and that they could move into it anytime after noon. They agreed to return in two hours; that would give them time to move their belongings out of their single rooms, because some new arrivals would be moving in.

The morning was spent strolling around St. George's Island looking at the shops. The sun soon warmed the air, so they both shed their sweaters and rolled up their sleeves. They found a bookstore that stocked books published in England, and Christopher bought one by his favorite author—the title hadn't been published in the States yet.

"This bookstore reminds me of one I used to visit in Oxford," he recalled absently.

"You remember that?"

"I suppose I must, I never really thought about it until now. Or was it something Stella told me?" he wondered. "She tried to fill in what she knew about my life for me after the accident. I know she was trying to be helpful, but it actually made things more difficult, because I couldn't be sure if I was really remembering certain things or if I just remembered her telling me about them. It gets rather confusing," he confessed.

"I imagine so," she agreed.

They returned to the Hilltop with a bottle of lime after-shave that Karyn had bought Christopher. She didn't tell him her secret intention of stealing some for herself. The plastic bag she carried, with one of the boutique's names slashed across it in bold colors, contained a blue-leather clutch purse he had bought her.

They were let into their new room promptly at noon. Located at the front of the house, it was bright and cheerful with large windows facing the bay. A four-poster double bed was covered with a lace spread that looked handmade. Matching doilies adorned a large bureau with an attached mirror. The warm furnishings lent an air of hominess to the room. Karyn was pleased to see that the bathroom contained a bathtub with a shower fixture.

By mutual agreement they unpacked most of their things right away, after first checking to see who had preferences about top or bottom drawers and left or right sides of the closet. They had a quick, carryout lunch of fish-and-chips in St. George before deciding to be daring and take the bus all the way to the opposite end of the island. On their tour with Vernon, they'd only gone as far as the Gibbs Hill Lighthouse and had not gone into Sandys or Somerset Parishes.

The bus ride was long—the low speed limit and frequent stops being the principal reasons. Masses of colorful bougainvillaea decorated the landscape. The bus followed a different route from the one Vernon had taken them on, so they were able to see more of the island. While the route wasn't as scenic as those along the shoreline, it was culturally interesting in that it showed the Bermudian communities and their way of everyday life. They were struck by

90

the cleanliness and high standard of living found through-out the island. There were no shacks for the poor or piles of garbage strewn around the land.

They stayed on the bus all the way to the end of the line—the Maritime Museum at the northwestern tip of Bermuda. After looking around at the interesting exhibits they caught the next bus back and stopped off in Somerset. This end of the island was very quiet and was visited by comparatively few tourists. There weren't many shops in town, but the few there were had wooden boardwalks fronting them.

They stopped at Mangrove Bay and enjoyed the sun-spangled view. A small group of anchored vessels bobbed in the quiet cove. Two tones of water-marked shoals near the shore and greater depths seaward. The striking, varie-gated effect was part of the natural beauty of Bermuda. It was too chilly for swimming, so they sat on the rock wall at the end of the beach and soaked up the peaceful atmo-sphere.

Glancing at his watch some time later, Christopher told her that they should be getting back because he had a special evening planned for them. Seeing Karyn's blush, he gently scolded her, "Naughty, naughty, that's not what I meant!" which made her blush even more.

Back at the Hilltop they entered their room together. Karyn nervously went over to admire the view from their window.

"Where are we going tonight?" she asked him without turning around.

"We'll be going out to dinner."

"What should I wear?"

"Something romantic," he suggested hopefully.

She walked over to the closet and was surveying her wardrobe when she felt his arms steal around her from behind. Karyn couldn't prevent herself from nervously stiffening. He felt her unresponsive reaction and slowly turned her in his arms. One look at her slightly pale face and downcast eyes was sufficient to make him draw her to the bed, where he sat her down before dropping next to her.

"Relax. I'm not going to hurt you," he placated her. Taking her hand in his he began to absently play with her fingers as he searched for the right words to allay her fears.

"The fact that we're married doesn't mean that we no longer have any privacy. We still have rights as individuals. So if you want privacy while you're changing, please feel free to use the bathroom. You won't hurt my feelings."

Christopher's sensitivity and support warmed her heart and melted the coldness caused by her anxieties.

"I love you," she whispered as she kissed him.

"You're just saying that so you can have the bathroom first," he blithely mocked her.

"Caught again!" she laughed.

This time she was smiling as she went to the closet and pulled out an soft apricot Indian cotton dress with an off-the-shoulder tie-string top and drawstring waist that fell into three tiers of ruffles. If it was romantic he wanted, romantic he would get! She put the dress over her arm and took her makeup bag with her into the bathroom.

The dress was a dream to wear, the soft material lovingly draping her figure. She had been nervous when she'd realized that she didn't have a strapless bra to wear with an off-the-shoulder style, but the blouson bodice hid her unhampered state from all but the most discerning eye. The pale apricot color enhanced her tanned shoulders and arms. Since coming to Bermuda, her color had deepened to a light brown, and even the bright red of her sunburn had faded to a warm tan.

Now for her hair. Karyn contemplated several styles before settling on a topknot with soft tendrils falling down to curl onto her cheeks and neck. She added a light brushing of bronze eye shadow to her lids, then highlighted it with a peach shadow under her brows. Her lashes were darkened with a touch of mascara and her lips outlined with an apricot lip gloss. She had left her sandals in the bedroom, so she gathered up her discarded jeans and shirt before opening the bathroom door.

Surprised to see Christopher shrugging into his suit jacket, she stood there for a moment, enjoying the sight of him. His muscular physique and sultry sexuality were a potent combination. He turned at her entrance, his eyes doing a slow perusal that encompassed her entire body. She felt as though he were touching her with his eyes, for they lingered over her bare shoulders and narrow waist with a startling tangibility before lowering to her long legs.

"You look good enough to eat," he reported huskily.

Karyn gave a small, shaky laugh. "You do and you'll spoil your appetite."

"Did you say appetite? Come closer, little girl, and I'll show you all about my 'appetites,' " he growled, throwing her a rakish look.

She cautiously stayed where she was, giving him an uncertain look that made him laugh. "I never seduce women on an empty stomach," he teasingly informed her, "so you're safe enough for the time being!"

She gave an exaggerated sigh of mock relief.

As Christopher hurried her down the stairs a few minutes later, she realized that she still had no idea where they were going, or how they were getting there. She was enlightened a bit when she discovered Vernon's car waiting for them on the other side of the garden gate. He cheerfully greeted them and they set off for their unknown destination.

It turned out to be one of the oldest restaurants in Bermuda. The moment Karyn walked into the dining room she could feel the romantic aura emanating from the room. Candles on each of the tables supplied the only lighting. The restaurant was in a restored inn right along the shore in Southampton Parish. Some of the guests were arriving by small launch at the private dock, which they could see through the window. Their table had an excellent location overlooking the necklace of islands that were strewn across the Little Sound with the glimmering lights of Hamilton glowing in the distance. It was hard to imagine a more poetic setting.

The food turned out to be as good as the view. Karyn chose the Filet Stephanie, while Christopher had Bermuda fish. They didn't speak much during dinner, seeming content to exchange long, intimate glances filled with unspoken communications. After dinner he swept her onto the dance floor, where the music was slow and the lights were low. He put his arms around her, folding her to him. After the first dance the music was merely an excuse for their embrace. A dreamy, contented smile shaped Karyn's lips as they continued to glide around the dance floor.

All too soon Christopher told her that it was time to leave. He assisted her back into Vernon's car, and they drove on in the moonlight.

"Is this the road back to St. George?" she hazily questioned.

"No, we're going to see Bermuda by moonlight and go along the south shore," her husband whispered, before going on to divulge suggestive secret messages and endearments in her ear.

Vernon dropped them off at a deserted beach and waited while they got out to admire the play of moonlight across the rippling waves. They walked hand in hand some way along the beach, and when they were out of sight, Christopher pulled her to him. Karyn's body seemed to blend with his, her soft curves merging with his lean angles. His lips brushed hers in a series of maddeningly teasing kisses that left her yearning for more. Before she knew what was happening, Christopher had turned her around, and they were both heading back to Vernon's car.

They drove back to the guesthouse in contented silence, Karyn still dwelling on the feelings of the past few hours rather than on the night that was yet to come. In her bemused state it seemed as though the return trip was completed in no time at all, and they were soon in the intimate privacy of their own room.

Christopher's lips met hers as soon as the door closed, the room still enshrouded in darkness. When he took a few steps into the room, Karyn followed him, her silken arms stealing around his neck. At first she was content just to be in his arms, but as their passions spiraled, she soon became impatient at the material between them. Her fingers stopped tracing the outline of his rugged jaw and lowered to slowly undo the buttons of his shirt, exposing the broad expanse of bronzed chest. His lips were wandering along her throat and lower, to the shadows between her creamy breasts.

He muttered a protest as the material of her dress barred him from further exploration. His fingers deftly untied the drawstring. She heard his indrawn breath as her dress slid to her waist, revealing the alabaster paleness of her round breasts to his hungry view.

"You've been driving me crazy all night, wondering if you were wearing anything under that flimsy material." His voice rasped with excitement as he enjoyed free access to her softly alluring curves. Christopher muttered his encouragement as she imitated his actions by sliding the shirt and jacket off his powerful shoulders. She was rewarded by his gasp of pleasure as she kissed the base of his throat, feeling his body heat burning against her mouth before she ran the palms of her hands down his chest to cling to his waist. His caresses became fiercer as his desires were raised to a feverish pitch. Karyn was scarcely aware of his fingers loosening the drawstring belt, allowing her cotton dress to slither to the floor.

She felt as though she were floating and realized that Christopher was carrying her to the bed. He gently laid her down and swiftly removed the few remaining barriers between them. The bed sagged as his weight joined hers on the soft mattress, and she felt the hard contours of his stimulating masculine body beside her.

Anxiety intruded as she wondered if she would be able to satisfy him, since she had never been with a man before and was traversing unfamiliar terrain. She found herself whispering her fears to her husband, seeking reassurance.

"You're gorgeous and I love you," he passionately murmured against the vulnerable hollows of her throat, his voice hoarse with desire. "I'll be as gentle as I can."

His mouth returned to hers with impelling urgency, his hands increasing the tempo of his caresses. Karyn was caught up in a swirling eddy of passion as she experienced her first moment of intense sexual excitement, burning with undreamed-of longings. She responded instinctively to his practiced hands educating her in the language of love, arching against his throbbing body as the disturbing ache in her lower limbs increased. Christopher carefully took her, and lowering his cheek to hers, tenderly kissed the tears of pain from her face.

She awoke very early in the morning, at first unable to place where she was. She felt an unfamiliar weight across her waist and realized that Christopher's arm held her to him, his hand gently resting on the curve of her breast. His features looked young and rather vulnerable in repose. She quietly slipped out of bed, careful not to disturb him.

As she soaked in a warm bath in the next room, Karyn reflected on her initiation into womanhood and wondered if something was wrong with her. While she had enjoyed her husband's initial lovemaking and was aroused by his fondling, she had felt the final consummation was disappointing. She was glad that Christopher had enjoyed the act, but felt a kind of envy for the satisfaction that he seemed to experience. All in all, she couldn't understand what all the hoopla was about.

Her meditation was interrupted by her husband knocking at the bathroom door before entering the room. He'd wrapped a robe around himself, apparently in a hurry, for he was still belting it when he walked in.

"I woke up and you weren't there. I was afraid you'd left or something. Poor baby, you didn't have as enjoyable a night as you'd hoped for, did you?" he sympathized. "But don't worry, the best is yet to come." Then, noticing the goose bumps on her arms, he briskly took a towel which hung on the rack and ordered, "Come on out, before you catch cold in there."

Karyn hesitated a moment before she complied, relieved to see that he quickly wrapped the towel around her, enclosing her arms within its fluffy warmth. Her relief disappeared when she felt his wandering hands along the line of her spine within the confines of the towel. Her arms were still enclosed, preventing her from protesting.

She felt the now familiar sensations quivering through her body. How could she feel this way when she knew what it would lead to? she asked herself in vain. His lips played with hers in between leisurely roving across her upturned face and neck. With a flick of his hands he slid the towel around, so that it was now wrapped across her back, and her damp naked body was pressed against his virile form.

"Your robe is getting wet," she protested halfheartedly.

"So take it off," he prompted her huskily.

He led her back to their bed as she did so. "This time will be much better," his deeply seductive voice promised her. "Just close your eyes and concentrate on what you're feeling."

She followed his direction and felt his hands softly mov-

97

ing over her, rhythmically stroking her with infinite care and precision, her body tingling under his educated fingers. She gasped with astonished delight as his passionate mouth ravished her, mapping out every inch of her body from shoulder to curving waist. She was shaken with wild tremors as he drove her crazy with his distracting lovemaking, methodically arousing her until she was consumed by such an intolerable hunger that it demanded satisfaction. Her palpitating body twisted uncontrollably beneath his.

"Now, darling, now," she moaned frantically, pulling him to her with delirious abandonment. She felt an outburst of ravishing relief when he finally took her, before drowning in a whirlpool of erotic sensations. Wave after wave of delicious feeling fluctuated through her body while she held him in the grip of passion.

It took some time for them to descend from the heights the climax of their possession had brought them to. So *this* is what all the hoopla is about, Karyn thought to herself with a languorous smile. Now she understood the full meaning of the words "making love." You could get addicted to it. Exhausted by the surge of emotion, they both drifted off to sleep, still clasped in a loose embrace.

The next time Karyn opened her eyes, the sun was high in the sky and shining into their room. Christopher was just waking up as she placed a warm kiss on the corner of his mouth.

"Good morning, husband," she shyly greeted him.

"Mmmm, good morning, wife." His sleepy voice was laced with intimacy. "Was it better last time?"

Her flushed but radiant face and brilliant smile warmed his heart, and his blood, when she confessed in wonderment, "Much better. Was it as fantastic for you as it was for me?"

"Indescribable!" he sighed. His vibrant blue eyes

gleamed with devilment as he declared, "It must be a case of practice making perfect, so . . ."

Her luminous green eyes widened in surprise before closing completely, shutting out everything except him. As things turned out, they missed breakfast and feasted on their love instead.

CHAPTER SIX

Those last days in Bermuda flew past as they toured the island by day and visited the realms of ecstasy at night. Christopher was a perfect lover who would often vary his approach, alternately seducing, cajoling, or intoxicating her. Karyn, in turn, gained confidence in her own sexuality as he tutored her in the art of making love, resulting in more pleasure for both of them.

All too soon, the time came for them to pack their belongings and end their idyllic interlude. After seeing the way Christopher jammed things into the case, Karyn took over and sent him to take care of the bill. She didn't hear him quietly enter the room. Seemingly engrossed with folding one of his shirts, she was actually worrying about their forthcoming separation. Thus, she was surprised to feel his hand cupping her cheek before turning her to face him.

"Sad to be going back?"

She silently nodded.

"Me too. But I'll call you every night, and hopefully, the two weeks will soon be over. Then we'll be together forever. You'll be so busy tidying up all those loose ends in Seattle that you probably won't even miss me, while I'll be moping around my house, inconsolable," he lamented theatrically.

"So I won't miss you, eh?" She moved closer and took up a threatening stance. "I shall definitely miss this," she paused to stroke his lips with hers, "and this," as her fingers snuck between the buttons of his crisp, blue shirt to gently trace imaginary designs along his warm skin. When he reached out to pull her closer, she rose on her toes to fit her body more intimately with his.

Christopher reluctantly set her from him. "We don't want to succumb to temptation and miss our flight."

"I suppose not," she agreed.

He snapped the cases shut, while Karyn did a last-minute check of the room, making sure that nothing was being left behind. This was the room where she had truly become his wife, and she felt as if they were taking a step from a safe place off into the unknown. She tried to shake the disturbing feeling as they rode in the cab to the airport. Vernon was working today and was unable to drive them, so they'd exchanged farewells over the phone, promising to call him the next time they came to Bermuda.

Stepping out of the cab at the airport, Karyn stood gazing at the brilliant azure waters of Castle Harbour, trying to memorize the scene in her mind. It was so beautiful here, so calm and peaceful. Bermuda's unspoiled natural setting made it a romantic paradise come true. The only thing lacking was the serpent, for one of the oddities of the island's natural history is the fact that there are no snakes. They sat outside on one of the benches facing the harbor until they could delay their departure no longer.

Their luggage had already been checked through. Fortunately, Karyn's flight to Seattle was on the same airline, so she wouldn't have to worry about her things until she arrived. She was surprised to see that they cleared U.S. Customs in Bermuda, before entering the departure lounge.

"That certainly saved time," Christopher commented, recalling long lines he had had to wait in.

Once in the departure lounge they had a few minutes before their flight was called, so they looked around the duty-free shops. Karyn stopped in the washroom, and she heard their flight being called as she emerged. At the top of the metal steps leading to the plane, she paused to turn around and savor her last look at Bermuda. There, past the square airport building at the end of the broad expanse of tarmac, was a chromatic streak of iridescent water. Bidding a silent farewell, Karyn ducked her head and followed her husband into the jet.

With a surge of energized power the plane lifted from the runway. The entire town of St. George lay beneath them, the gleaming white roofs atop pastel-colored buildings growing smaller as the jet gained altitude. Heading out over the open sea, she was able to look down and see the coral reefs through the clear, sparkling, blue-green water.

They had an uneventful flight, landing on time at Chicago's O'Hare International Airport, the busiest in the world. She waited with Christopher while he picked up his luggage in the baggage claim area and stored it in a nearby locker because he intended seeing her to her continuing flight. They had a little over an hour to wait, and they spent it in the departure lounge at the gate, quietly holding hands.

A growing tumult of anxiety churned within her, a million "what if's" running through her head. Was she doing the right thing in going on to Seattle? Yet what choice was there? Susan couldn't be expected to do all the work the move entailed.

As the time drew nearer, Karyn found she didn't know what to say. A paralyzing apprehension had taken hold of her tongue, cleaving it to the roof of her mouth. When her flight was called, she was one of the last to board, trying to put off that dreaded moment of separation.

"You'll meet me at the airport on the twenty-ninth, right? And you'll call me every night; you haven't lost my number, have you?" She wanted to add "you won't forget" but was reluctant to bring up that sensitive subject.

"Yes, I'll meet you at the airport, and yes, I have your number and will call you every night." His low voice held a teasing inflection that was belied by the grim seriousness of his eyes.

"It's two hours earlier in Seattle," she reminded him.

"I know." He gathered her close for a final embrace, their lips merging in a flaming kiss.

She fastened her seatbelt while the plane was taxiing out to the runway, warmly recalling her husband's last whispered words, "I love you, and I won't forget you." Tucked into the side pocket of her handbag was a small box that Christopher had handed her on their flight from Bermuda, after obtaining her promise that she wouldn't open it until she got to her apartment.

During the long flight, Karyn's thoughts strayed to her friend Susan's reactions to her news of moving to Chicago. She felt twinges of guilt because she hadn't even really considered Susan's feelings and was almost leaving her in the lurch. Of course, Karyn would continue to pay her share of the rent until the lease was up, or until Susan found another roommate, but she couldn't compensate Susan for her absence.

So it was with some slight trepidation that Karyn stepped off the plane in Seattle. They caught sight of each other right away, and Susan hurried over to help Karyn with her hand luggage, her round face aglow with welcome.

"How was the vacation?" Susan asked her after hugging her briefly. "You look so tanned and healthy that I'm absolutely green with envy!" Susan was a very outgoing sort of person and kept up a running chatter all the way to her car. As she pulled out onto the expressway, she told Karyn, "I have a surprise for you back at the apartment."

And I have one for you, Karyn thought to herself, keeping her fingers crossed that her friend would understand. She didn't feel she could really relax until they had arrived at the apartment and she had dropped her cases in her room.

"Would you like something to drink, some tea or coffee?" Susan asked her. "It must seem rather chilly for you after the warm breezes in Bermuda."

Karyn shook her head and sat down on the couch. "No thanks, Susan, but I would like to talk to you."

When Susan sat down, they turned to each other and simultaneously began, "You won't believe what happened." They broke off in amazement at their echoing statements before doubling over with laughter.

"You first," Susan said.

"No, you begin," Karyn prompted.

"Darryl proposed," Susan burst out, naming the man she had been dating for almost a year.

Karyn stared at her in surprise. "I thought you said that he was just a friend, strictly a platonic relationship. He wasn't the type to give you . . . 'romantic notions' is the way I think you put it."

Susan blushed. "Yes, well that was then. All of a sudden I looked at him and thought 'I'd like to spend the rest of my life with you.' You know, I've been falling in and out of love quite frequently with all these dashing types who have the characters of squids. The last time it happened I thought to myself, 'Susan, why do you keep hurting yourself like this? It's pretty stupid to do that to yourself when you know a special human being whom you can really trust and to whom you can relate.' So we're relating!" she ended up with a laugh.

Karyn had to laugh with her. Oh, what a relief. It was true that her friend had been going from one unreliable man to another during the past year, seeming to pick the same type over and over again, ending up hurt each time. Darryl was completely different; she approved wholeheartedly of her friend's choice—and their forthcoming marriage would make her own departure much less painful.

"Well, aren't you going to say something?" Susan demanded.

"Of course. I approve one hundred percent," Karyn told her. "You couldn't have made a better decision."

"Thank you. I think so too!" her friend said irrepressibly. "Now, what's your news?"

"You'll never guess who I met in Bermuda!"

"Is he tall, dark, and handsome?"

"Yes."

"Burt Reynolds!" she cried, naming her own favorite movie star.

"No," Karyn laughed.

Susan thought a moment and then looked at Karyn's glowing face uncertainly.

"Not Christopher?"

"Yes!"

"But how? . . . What?" Susan sputtered.

Karyn told her the entire story: how Christopher had been the victim of an accident resulting in his amnesia; Stella's involvement with his move to Milwaukee; and his uncle's death, requiring a transfer to Chicago to run the business.

"But what about you? Why did he remember almost everything else about his life and not you?" Susan demanded.

"He also can't remember the night he disappeared," Karyn reminded her. "And I don't know why he forgot me. I'm going to speak to his doctor when I get to Chicago."

"You're just going to give up your job and everything to fly to Chicago to live with him?" Susan asked in amazement.

"He's my husband, and I love him very much. Wouldn't you do the same thing if you were in my place?"

Susan pondered the question carefully before a grin broke out across her face, lighting her dark-brown eyes. "I can't see Darryl suffering from amnesia or getting involved with anything mysterious," she confessed. Karyn had to agree—Darryl was the armchair type. "I suppose if it did happen, I would do the same. But this Stella woman sounds pretty shady to me. Is she still involved in Christopher's life?"

"He said she comes down to Chicago every now and then and that he would like to see her married to a friend of his."

"Poor friend," Susan decided. Karyn had to agree. "Well, be careful when you size her up. Don't underestimate the enemy," Susan advised.

"I won't," Karyn promised.

Later that evening when she spoke to her parents on the phone, she wished her mother could've shown the same kind of acceptance Susan had.

"You're what?" her mother's shocked voice came over the line.

"I'm moving to Chicago."

"With Christopher?"

"He is my husband," she reminded her.

"But he deserted you!" Karyn winced at the vehemence of her mother's statement.

"Mother, I explained about his loss of memory."

"Yes, I know you did. I'm not the one with amnesia," Mrs. Kadik sniped bitterly. "I never heard such a load of garbage in all my life. Of all the lame excuses. 'Oh forgive me, dear, I forgot I was married,' " she mimicked cruelly.

"I told you that Christopher was hurt in the accident; he still has a scar on his forehead and hand." She decided not to mention the scar she had discovered on his right hip their second night together. Her lips were parted in a contented smile as she recalled the scene in her mind's eye.

She'd been kissing him, savoring the feel of him when

her fingertips had discovered the scar running about five inches along the length of his right hip.

"What happened to you?"

"I told you; it's from the accident." His answer was muffled by her hair.

"You told me about your head and hand, not your hip."

"I thought I'd let you discover that one for yourself," he had teased her. "What are you laughing at?"

"I just realized as I said it that all your scars are on parts of your body starting with an *h*. Very good planning," she applauded him.

"I also have a scar on my heart, but you've healed that with your love."

"Karyn!" Her mother's strident voice brought her out of her daydream.

"Yes?"

"I asked you if you were in trouble."

"Trouble?" she repeated, confused.

"I mean, he didn't attack you or anything, did he? Is he forcing you to live with him in Chicago?"

"Mother, I'm going of my own free will because I love him and he loves me. Nothing has changed."

"How can you say that after what he's done to you!" her mother wailed.

"I hope you'll understand once you've grown used to the idea."

"I'm going to talk to your father," Mrs. Kadik decided. "I think we should come to Chicago to make sure you're all right and that Christopher isn't mad or anything. You know, if he really had that accident, it could have scrambled his brains. He could become dangerous! I'll have your father check into that with Dr. Kern."

"Look Mother, I have to go now. I'll call you when I get to Chicago. Give my love to Daddy."

After hanging up, Karyn gave a sigh of relief because that difficult chore was over. Christopher's call later that evening helped wipe out some of the uneasiness caused by her mother's call.

"Did you open my present yet?" he asked her.

"Yes, thank you," thinking of the pewter bicycle stickpin. "When did you get it?"

"I went back to the shop at the airport while you were in the washroom."

"Clever! Was it supposed to remind me of the day we tried to get a moped?"

"Yes. Since I couldn't find a bike for you then, I thought it only fair to get you one later!" reminding her of the trouble they'd encountered trying to hire a moped. Both of them had ended up laughing when they'd found out that the only thing the shop had left was a giant old-fashioned bicycle and had decided to do something else for the day. Recalling what that something was, Karyn's blood warmed.

"I remember," she said huskily.

"Is everything going all right? Did you tell Susan and call your parents?"

"Yes to both questions," she answered.

"Well, what were their reactions?" he demanded.

She explained Susan's good news and tried to gloss over her mother's reaction as much as possible.

"I sort of suspected she wouldn't be pleased," Christopher confessed. "I hope she didn't upset you."

"No. My goodness, I almost forgot this is a long-distance call. Are you sure you can afford to phone me every night?" Karyn asked in concern. "Maybe we should make it every other night."

"I wouldn't be able to survive!" he moaned dramatically. "Don't worry about it," he went on to reassure her. "I've got enough money to take care of the phone bill, and I am calling during the lower evening rates. But it's nice to know that I've got a practical wife," he told her.

"Practical?" she queried.

"Practically perfect," he elaborated.

"What's between me and perfection?" she questioned.

"The fact that you're too far away!" he complained.

On that note they said good-bye, with Christopher promising to call her at the same time the next day.

CHAPTER SEVEN

The next two weeks were jammed full of activity as Karyn gave notice at work and tried to get all her belongings packed at home. She'd also wanted to make some purchases of things from the Far East, which were more reasonably priced in Seattle than they would be in Chicago, if available there at all. There were people to say good-bye to, library books to return, accounts to be closed, and the million-and-one little details that take so long. Karyn was almost too busy to really contemplate the move until her last day at work.

Her fellow employees had arranged a surprise farewell party for her, and Karyn's throat was tight with pent-up emotion at the many kindnesses shown to her by her friends. One of the other secretaries had baked a cake and decorated it to say "Good luck, Karyn!" Several other people gave her small gifts, such as perfume or stationery . . . "So you can write us all the way from the Windy City!" she was told. Her boss presented her with a bonus and a glowing reference. Karyn expressed her last farewells reluctantly, promising to keep in touch.

By the time she reached home, she was ready to shed a few tears at the closing of this chapter in her life. She'd been in Seattle for just over a year and had been working all that time with the same law firm. Some of the old doubts came back to plague her, only partially dispelled by Christopher's phone call later that evening.

On Karyn's last night Susan and Darryl took her to one of the fanciest restaurants in town. After an enjoyable meal of fresh seafood, they talked until long after midnight, enjoying each other's company and realizing that it would be some time before they could get together again. Karyn had spent the greater part of that day trying to jam the last few things into her suitcase, and she and Susan had both ended up sitting on the cases in order to get them shut.

She'd never realized how many clothes she'd bought while in Seattle. Of course, clothes were a great morale booster, and her morale had been at rock bottom when she'd first arrived at Susan's apartment. Not that Karyn had been terribly extravagant—a majority of the things she'd acquired had been on sale, and she'd been making a good salary as a legal secretary, without many expenses besides rent and food. She definitely wouldn't be coming to Christopher with just the shirt on her back, although he might actually prefer her without it, she thought to herself with a grin, recalling those last days in Bermuda they'd spent together as husband and wife.

At the airport the next day she had an emotional leave-taking with Susan. Both women ended up crying, laughing, and hugging each other all at the same time, interspersed with promises to write often and to visit each other soon. Karyn felt quite drained by the time she boarded the plane to Chicago. There had been a hazy quality about the last few days, as if they had been filmed through the distorted lens of a camera.

Christopher's call the night before had been short. He was having problems at work and hadn't gotten home until late. The line hadn't been very clear either, so they'd been brief, saying they'd meet tomorrow. Karyn had changed her outfit three times before settling on the slim navy-blue skirt with buttons down the side and a matching jacket. Her blouse was gold- and blue-checked cotton,

111

comfortable for traveling. She wore blue-leather sandals and the navy clutch that Christopher had given her in Bermuda.

When Mount Rainier came into view above the cloud cover, Karyn waved a mental good-bye to one of her favorite landmarks of her adopted city. Returning to the Midwest, where the plains stretched out for hundreds of miles without end, she would miss the rugged scenery of the Northwest. She'd always enjoyed the great variety of landscape to be found in such proximity to Seattle. Karyn had often gone to Puget Sound and watched the many ships sailing or cruising across the water. She and Susan had even taken an excursion to the Olympic Peninsula, where she'd gazed in awe at the huge range of mountains. It had been amazing to find that there was a rain forest only a short distance away.

The jet encountered a low-pressure front over the Rockies, and the accompanying storms and turbulence delayed her flight's arrival in Chicago by one hour. Once the plane taxied to the assigned gate and engines were turned off, Karyn gathered her belongings, anxiously hoping that Christopher had called the airline to confirm the arrival time and discovered the delay instead of wasting all that time hanging around the airport.

She followed the other passengers as they walked down the long tunnel connecting the plane to the terminal. Side-stepping the embracing couple ahead of her Karyn scanned the crowd for her husband's face. There was no sign of him. Her stomach, already rather queasy from the rough flight, sank alarmingly.

She left the heavy traffic area and sat down on one of the chairs lining the wall of the waiting lounge. Perhaps the airline had thought her plane would be later than it actually was, she reasoned with herself. Or perhaps Christopher got tired of waiting and went to get a bite to eat, since it was nearing dinner time. But another silent voice taunted her with the supposition that he might never show up, like the last time they were in Chicago. For the most part she was able to drown out those thoughts with the calmer voice of reason. But as the hands on her watch continued to make their way around the small gold face, she found it harder and harder to suppress that taunting voice.

Her emotions swung from anger to confusion and fear. Where was he? Why make all the arrangements for her to come here and then not show up? Didn't he realize how she'd feel, what she'd think? Or didn't he care?

After waiting for nearly an hour Karyn gathered her belongings together again. That made it a total of two hours past the scheduled arrival time, she calculated despairingly. Now what should I do? The answer came swiftly. The logical thing would be to call him. You should've done that right away, she mentally chastised herself while digging in her purse for change.

The public telephones were some distance away, and she had to stop every so often to shift her heavy hand luggage from one hand to another. Leaning down in front of the payphones she was trying to unhook the stubborn strap of her carryall from her shoulder when a fast-moving figure caught her bag with a blow that would've sent her sprawling if she hadn't steadied herself by catching hold of the side of the phone counter. Karyn glared in outrage at the rapidly departing back of the figure dashing down the hallway. Probably some businessman late for a flight, she thought to herself in disgust.

There was no answer at Christopher's house. She tried to smother her disappointment and rising fears by reasoning that no answer could mean that he was on his way. Turning away from the booth, Karyn was trying to decide what her next course of action would be when she saw the lone figure waiting at the gate where her flight had arrived. The first thing she noticed was that it was the man who

113

had nearly knocked her down and the second thing she noticed was that it was her husband!

Irritation at the rude behavior of the stranger was swiftly replaced by a flood of relief at Christopher's appearance. She slowly walked up to him, her approach out of his line of vision. Her things were left in a pile a few feet away, and Karyn continued until she was directly behind him. She put out her arms and wrapped them around his waist, surprised to feel his body trembling. Only then did she realize that while she had been worried that he wouldn't show, Christopher had been worrying the same thing about her. He turned immediately and gathered her close in a tight embrace.

"Where have you been?" he demanded unsteadily.

"Where have I been?" she repeated. "Where have you been? My flight landed over an hour ago."

"Stella gave me the wrong arrival time."

"Stella!" she exclaimed, a sick feeling knotting the pit of her stomach. At the sound of that woman's name her anger returned.

"Look, I'll explain later. Let's get your things and head for home." Christopher easily picked up her hand luggage while Karyn followed him, envying the ease with which he carried the heavy cases. The long walk to the baggage claim area gave her a chance to calm herself, holding on to her temper. They didn't have a chance to talk again until they were downstairs, looking for her luggage.

"You never answered my question," he reminded her, while an airline representative went to check where her suitcases might be, since all the other passengers on her flight had long gone with their own. "Where were you?"

Keep it cool, she instructed herself. Don't let Stella ruin your homecoming. "Actually, I was calling the house to see where you were, but before I could deposit my twenty cents, some maniac came running down the hall and nearly knocked me over!"

"Are you okay?"

"Yes, I'm okay, but I sure felt like slugging the guy. Luckily for you, I got over my thirst for bloody revenge!"

"Luckily for me?" Christopher questioned blankly before realization dawned. "It was you I ran into when I was dashing to the gate. I didn't realize . . ."

"So I gathered," she laughed at the contrition on his handsome face. "I didn't think it was a very nice way to welcome me to Chicago. Unique, yes. Nice, no."

"I'm sorry," he apologized automatically. "I was afraid of missing you. When I got to the gate and it was deserted, I didn't know what to do," he confessed grimly.

"I know," she said softly. "I felt the same way."

The airline representative came back, triumphantly carrying the two suitcases in his hands like the winner of a treasure hunt.

"Here they are, sir. They were set aside in the unclaimed baggage area."

Once Karyn had comfortably settled herself in Christopher's car, she inquired, "Now, what's this about Stella?" Her voice, she was proud to note, reflected none of her inner agitation.

"You remember me telling you about my secretary?" he prompted.

"No. You told me you were having problems at work, but nothing specific."

"Oh, well it was my secretary. She quit without giving any notice, just up and left. Stella happened to be in town at the time and offered to step in while I looked around for a replacement."

"Whatever happened to temporary help?" she retorted resentfully. "And I thought Stella was a nurse."

"She is, but she's been having problems with her job. It seems her boss is an older woman who's extremely jealous of Stella and makes life very difficult for her."

I'll bet, Karyn thought to herself. Poor Stella.

"As for temporary help," he continued, "I suppose I could have called an agency, but after Stella offered, it would have been rude to turn her down. I think she and Bob may be closer to coming to an understanding. I'm sure you'll be good friends," he ended.

Oh no, Karyn inwardly shook her head at that idea. Their conversation lagged, and silence reigned for most of the drive. She felt awkward and uneasy after their anti-climactic meeting at the airport. This wasn't going according to plan at all. Her tremulous expectations had gone flat.

The sun was beginning to set when they drove up the small driveway leading to an attached garage. In the rosy light of dusk stood a modern A-frame with natural wood siding. The house had a lovely location, situated on the end of a cul-de-sac with a large expanse of woods behind it. A measure of her eager anticipation returned. Christopher helped her out of the car and retained her hand as he lead her toward the front door.

After he unlocked it, she was startled to feel him scooping her up in his arms and carrying her over the threshold. Karyn barely had time to clasp her arms around his neck before he set her down again, slowly letting her body slide against the lean length of his.

"Welcome to your new home, Mrs. Reid." The formal greeting was delivered with a husky tenderness. He lowered his lips to hers to bestow a slow, gentle kiss that warmed her heart, and other parts of her anatomy, as his kiss deepened, reflecting his urgent need. Her pleasure was rudely interrupted by the sense of another presence. Karyn opened her eyes to find a petite, blond woman standing in the doorway behind them, glaring at her with unconcealed hatred.

She stepped back, surprised at both Stella's sudden appearance and the obvious intensity of her animosity, for this must be Stella! Who else would have the nerve to enter the house unannounced? Karyn's sudden withdrawal was explained when he heard Stella speaking behind him.

"Chris, dear! I'm so sorry to interrupt. You know I wouldn't have intruded for the world, but I just found out that I'd given you the wrong time for Karyn's arrival, and I wanted to make sure that you'd met her all right. I can see you have," flinging a barbed look at Karyn that went undetected by Christopher. "When I called the airlines the stupid girl on the phone had an awful cold, and I couldn't understand a word she said. It's been so busy in the office that I never got around to calling back to confirm it until you'd already left. I came right over as soon as I discovered my mistake. I probably should've called first, but you know how I rush into things when the people I . . ." she gave a breathless laugh, "care about are concerned."

Karyn could only stand there, amazed at the ease and speed with which the other woman had changed her tune. Yet, she was sure that the change was only surface-deep, knowing that she hadn't misinterpreted Stella's first venomous look. Her ash-blond hair was shorn fashionably short, the style accentuating the hardness of her perfectly made-up face. Judging from the worldly knowledge in those china-blue eyes, she presumed Stella's age to be close to Christopher's twenty-nine.

Christopher made the introductions. "Stella, I'd like you to meet my wife, Karyn. Karyn, this is Stella. I told you about her."

"I'm so glad to meet you," Stella falsely enthused. After Karyn made some quiet response, Stella went on to intimately chide Christopher. "You really shouldn't be telling your wife about me. Don't you know that women don't like to hear about another woman, at least not from a man," she qualified with a smirk. "Now I'll leave you two newlyweds alone, and I'll close the door after me. We don't want you shocking the neighbors, do we?" leaving Karyn with the feeling that they had been involved in some kind of illicit behavior in the middle of the street rather than kissing in their own home. With a gay wave and "I'll see you tomorrow, Chris" Stella made her exit.

Karyn found the unsettling feeling hard to shake as Christopher gave her a tour of the house. The downstairs was comprised of a spacious living room that continued on into a dining room. The floor was covered with a deep plush chocolate-brown wall-to-wall carpet; the walls were off-white. Across the hall was the kitchen, with a cheery breakfast nook. A small bathroom at the front of the house completed the tour of that floor. The upstairs only covered half the area of the downstairs, thereby allowing the living room and dining room to have an open cathedral ceiling crisscrossed by dark wooden beams. A brick fireplace was built into the far wall. The staircase going upstairs was open, and there was a small railing that enclosed the hall-way at the top, creating the effect of an internal balcony. Going down the hall upstairs, they passed another bath-room and a bedroom before her husband stopped in front of the door at the end of the hall.

"This is our room," he announced, opening the door with a flourish.

It was a large airy room with windows on two walls and a large double bed flanked by two teak cabinets along the third wall. A large closet partially covered the fourth wall, and a door next to it lead into a good-sized master bath-room. There was a comfortable chair in the corner, be-tween the two windows that looked out over the side of the house and back into the woods.

"It's lovely," Karyn enthused.

Christopher walked over to one of the matching cabi-nets and said, "This one is all yours. I went out the day after I got home and bought it. Fortunately, the Scan-dinavian import store still had them in stock. I like mine and find it very handy, so I thought you might want one of your own."

118

His thoughtfulness touched her. "Susan must've told you how many clothes I have, right?" she teased, unable to express her appreciation in any other way.

The floor was bare except for a few strategically placed wool rugs with geometric designs. "I hadn't decided what kind of rug to get for this room," he explained. "All I really did was buy myself the bare necessities," pointing to the drapes and matching bedspread in warm rust.

"You've done very well," she congratulated him. "It really is a beautiful house." Peering out into the darkening gloom, she inquired, "How far back does the lot go?"

Christopher came close to her and pointed out the trees marking the boundaries of the pie-shaped lot. "You'll be able to see them better in the morning."

Noticing the tenseness of her body as he stood close beside her, he decided to go down and bring up her cases so she could begin to settle in. Karyn tried to shed the disquieting feelings of uncertainty that had plagued her since Stella's unexpected visit. It wouldn't have been so bad if the meeting had taken place the following day; by then she would've felt a little more at ease in her new surroundings. But coming right after the news that Stella was working in her husband's office and his late arrival at the airport, it had been hard to handle.

Christopher brought up her cases and set them down with an exaggerated groan.

"You're going to need the extra room in that dresser if the weight of these is anything to go by."

"How do you know that I haven't brought a piece of Mount Rainier with me?"

"You'd need extra space to store that too," he pointed out logically.

After two trips he had all her belongings in the room and offered to make dinner while she unpacked.

"You've had a long day. If you want to take a bath, feel free." Christopher turned on the bathroom light and pointed out the almond bathtub. Karyn blushed when she remembered the tub in their bathroom in Bermuda and how he'd come in and found her there before teaching her the joys of love.

Mumbling an uneven thanks, she hurried over to her cases and began unpacking them, heaving a small sigh after he left the room. She explored the cupboards and drawers in the dresser, admiring the fine workmanship of the piece. The teakwood felt smooth beneath her slender fingers. Both suitcases were emptied and Karyn was hanging up her last dress in the roomy closet when she heard Christopher yell up the stairs, "Soup's on!"

She came downstairs to find her husband standing next to the dining room table. He had a white tea towel folded over his arm and was politely pulling the chair out for her.

"Would madame care for a before-dinner drink?" he inquired with an atrocious French accent.

"No, thank you," she answered politely.

"Well, zen, here is ze zoup!" uncovering the bowl in the middle of the table and ladling out some creamy mushroom soup into her bowl. It was tasty, and Karyn was lavish in her praise.

"I will tell ze chef," Christopher replied.

"I had no idea you could cook so well."

"Ooops, now I've let the cat out of the bag, haven't I. I'll be chained to the stove every night!"

His deliberately aghast expression made her giggle. The dinner was enjoyable. The main course was steak and mashed potatoes with a tossed salad. She decided against dessert and followed her husband into the kitchen where they both did the dishes, Karyn washing, Christopher drying and putting away.

"I do have a dishwasher," he announced after putting the last dish away.

"You can say that again," she agreed, wiping any trace of suds from the sink.

120

"No, I mean an automatic one." He indicated the built-in dishwasher underneath the counter.

"And you made me slave away for hours while you had that to work for you?" she accused him.

"I was trying to conserve energy," he protested.

"Not mine!"

They both ended up laughing and walked back into the living room, where Christopher put on a selection of music by Debussy and dimmed the lights.

"It's a shame it's too warm tonight for a fire. Come here and sit down next to me." He patted the oatmeal-colored couch seat. Karyn slowly complied. "Relax," he instructed, putting his arm around her. She closed her eyes and enjoyed the softly flowing strains of the music and the feel of his arm, warm on her shoulders. They listened to two more records, the selected discs dropping automatically. The enchanted music of Debussy relaxed her to the point of drowsiness. Christopher's low voice disrupted her somnolent peace. "Let's head for bed before you fall asleep right here." She immediately sat up, her heart pounding nervously. "Come on, no protesting. You go on up. I'll just make sure the doors are locked."

Karyn went upstairs and pulled a blue nightie from the drawer, taking it and her robe into the bathroom, where she changed. While brushing her teeth, she looked into the mirror and grimaced at the pale, uncertain reflection staring back at her. I look about sixteen and scared stiff, she noted in disgust. Why? The reason was simple, Stella. No longer a faceless shadow, the other woman haunted her thoughts. Karyn was unable to forget the look of venomous hatred Stella had thrown her. And that was before they'd even been introduced.

With a pensive sigh she unlocked and opened the bathroom door. Christopher had just come into the room, absently undoing his tie. He came close and placed a warm kiss along her cheek.

121

"Mmmm, you smell like lemon."

"It's the soap I just washed my face with," she said nervously, moving away to hang up her suit. He followed her to the closet.

"What's wrong?" he gently asked.

"I don't know what you mean," she protested.

He pulled her into his arms and began kissing her, but she was unable to respond. Had he ever kissed Stella like this? The unbidden question prevented her from reciprocating the embrace.

"That's what I mean." His voice was expressionless.

"I'm sorry. I think I must be very tired. It was a long and bumpy flight, and I was busy right up to the minute I got on the plane."

Christopher studied her face, trying to judge if she was telling the truth. She did look tired. "Hop into bed; you're home now and can get a good night's sleep."

Karyn climbed under the covers while he went into the bathroom, presumably to change. She'd only left one small lamp burning, which he turned out when he made his way to the bed. Feigning sleep, she felt him slide in on the other side. He leaned over her shoulder and murmured, "Good night, darling," before softly kissing her cheek. Then he settled into his own side of the bed.

Karyn was still awake long after she heard the steady rhythm of his breathing that told her he was asleep. She silently cursed Stella for ruining her first night home and then herself for letting the other woman affect her so much.

CHAPTER EIGHT

Karyn felt on top of the world, both literally and figuratively. The morning had begun with Christopher bringing her breakfast in bed before telling her that he wanted to give her a tour of Chicago, since it was Sunday and he didn't have to go to work. She resolved to forget Stella and enjoy the day with her husband.

They'd driven downtown and visited some of the famous landmarks of America's second largest city. Water Tower Place, an exclusive vertical shopping center enclosed within a high rise, was their first stop. A glass elevator glided them between the seven different levels. Across the street was the old Chicago Water Tower, the only thing left standing in that area after the Great Chicago Fire of 1871 destroyed most of the city.

They strolled down Michigan Avenue, looking in the windows of some of the world's most expensive shops. Farther south on Michigan Avenue was the Chicago Art Institute, where they lingered over the extensive Impressionist collection. Karyn only let herself be dragged away after extracting a promise from her husband that they would return and spend at least one full day there.

Going down Lake Shore Drive had been an unforgettable experience. Parks reminiscent of Paris lined the blue expanse of Lake Michigan, while billowy clouds of cotton puffs adorned the porcelain sky. An invigorating breeze, lacking the usual fumes one normally associates with a large city, blew through the car's open windows.

Christopher turned off onto the dead-end peninsula leading to the Adler Planetarium and parked there. Before them reared the spectacular skyline of Chicago, a unique and arresting array of structural monuments.

"See that tall white skyscraper over there?" he asked.

"Yes."

"That's the Standard Oil Building, the world's largest marble-covered building. The stone slabs came from Italy's Carrara Mountains, where Michelangelo got his marble."

"Michelangelo would have culture shock," Karyn humorously decided. "Chicago certainly has more than its fair share of fascinating buildings."

A picnic basket full of fruit and cheese was whisked out of the trunk. They chose a spot along the lake with the towering skyline as a backdrop. Her husband had promised that at their next stop they would "scale the heights," but would tell her no more.

"Are we going mountain climbing in Chicago?"

Christopher laughed and refused to be drawn out. "Where's your romantic spirit?" he teased her.

"Umm, this sounds interesting. Are you propositioning me here in the middle of the big city?"

"No, but that sounds like a good idea, too!"

Their hidden destination turned out to be the lofty Sears Tower, the tallest building in the world.

"I thought the World Trade Center in New York was the tallest," Karyn interjected.

"So do a lot of other people, but the Sears Tower is actually 104 feet taller!"

After riding the express elevator to the enclosed observation deck and admiring the view from the floor-to-ceiling windows, Karyn did feel as though they were on top of the world, with Chicago at their feet. Tiny dots of cars moved along narrow streets that demarcated the city into square blocks. The verdant forest-preserve system that encircled the city was visible on the outer ring of the metropolis. In the opposite direction was the harbor-studded lakeshore.

"Lake Michigan is the third largest of the five Great Lakes," Christopher informed her. "It is the only one that is entirely in the United States: the other four are shared with Canada."

An audiovisual exhibit about Chicago's history was set up on one end of the observation deck, and they stopped to view it. Afterward, Christopher began reading from the pamphlet he had picked up in the Visitor's Center on the main floor: " 'The Sears Tower is 110 stories, or 1454 feet high, and contains 4.5 million gross square feet of space. It took four years to complete and has 16,000 tinted windows and 28 acres of black duranodic aluminum skin. The 222,500-ton building is supported by 114 rock caissons, each one sunk as deep as the Statue of Liberty is tall. The tower contains enough telephone conductor wire to go around the world 1 ¾ times! There are 103 elevators, two of which are express elevators that can reach the observation deck in less than one minute . . . .' "

"My head is reeling from all those figures!" she theatrically exclaimed. "How many windows did you say there were?"

"Sixteen thousand," Christopher replied.

"How do you imagine they clean them all?"

"I don't have to imagine. I know! An automatic window-washing system cleans the exterior eight times a year."

"How many people do you think work here?"

"Twelve thousand."

"I should've known you would have all the answers, Dr. Reid," Karyn mocked him.

"Are you insinuating that I'm showing off?" he growled laughingly.

"No," she denied. "I'm interested."

"I'll finish today's lecture with the fact that the first steel, so-called skyscraper was built in Chicago in 1885 and consisted of eleven stories. We've come up in the world quite a bit since then!"

They stopped off at an Italian restaurant for a pizza on their way back home that evening. It was a small establishment and Christopher seemed to be a frequent customer, judging by the owner's welcome. A mouth-watering aroma of hot, fresh dough and spicy tomato sauce filled the air. The pizza was loaded with all the trimmings—sausage, mushrooms, green peppers—and dripping with cheese. Karyn washed it down with a frosty mug of root beer, while Christopher had beer.

By the time they got back home, the evening had turned quite chilly. Christopher knelt in front of the fireplace in their living room and within a few minutes, a cheerful fire was crackling. He settled in a comfortable leather chair, while Karyn rested on the floor, her knees bent, her arms across his thighs, and her back to the fire.

They sat in a companionable silence for some time, making infrequent comments about their day, until Christopher broke one of the long silences to growl mockingly, "That's where I like my women—at my feet!"

"Really?" she asked sweetly, before yanking him from his chair and pulling him down onto the floor next to her, where she rolled over on top of him. He blinked in surprise.

"You should have known that was a dangerous thing to say to a liberated woman," she reproved him.

Christopher quickly recovered. "Let's liberate you a little more, shall we?" he suggested wickedly, his attractive mouth slanting in a smile. He loosened her blouse and tugged her down to him so that he could kiss the creamy

126

expanse of skin he had just uncovered. Her limbs began to soften at the feel of his warm body pressed closely against hers.

His hands were running up and down the curvature of her spine, pausing to make special swirling motions in the small of her back. Their magic forced her body to compliantly curve into his. She parted her lips to whisper his name, only to have him swoop down to capture their sweetness before she could utter a word. It was as if he put a match to her, causing a raging fire between and within them.

Threading her hands through his soft brown hair, Karyn felt his chest contract in a sigh of pleasure when she rubbed her breasts against him. With languid assurance he rolled over so that his body enveloped hers, moving in earnest now to release the rest of her clothing.

Realizing his intent, she tore her mouth from his to protest, "Darling, not here!"

"Why not here?" Christopher urged her seductively, his breath intermingling with hers. "It couldn't be more romantic . . . what with the firelight, soft carpet, and . . ." his voice dropped to a sexy whisper, "you."

That firm, irresistible mouth returned to hers, their lips blending in an incandescent kiss that enticed her to comply. Karyn's inhibitions were eventually blown away as he stormed her senses and made her his. The longed-for fluctuation of erotic sensation coursed through her, while their shadows tangled on the wall behind them, outlining their convulsively writhing forms until the fire died out.

Karyn was still on cloud nine the following afternoon. Her housework was interspersed with long pauses, her dreamy green eyes frequently gazing off into space, remembering the events of the previous night with delectable clarity. When the phone rang, she rushed to answer it, hoping it would be Christopher. She couldn't have been more disappointed to hear Stella's crisp, self-confident voice on the line.

"Karyn, this is Stella."

"Yes," she answered cautiously.

"Chris seems most unlike himself this morning, very absent-minded. I hope you haven't been upsetting him," the other woman accused. "You know the doctor has given strict instructions that he's not to be exposed to any emotional stress. God knows, I'm trying to do my share by making things easier for him at the office, but you're ruining all my good work. What did you do to him last night?" she demanded.

Stella's accusatory tone made Karyn lose her temper. "That's none of your business. What goes on between a husband and wife is privileged information." She felt a momentary triumph at the astounded silence from the other end of the line.

Stella quickly regained her control. "So the gloves are off now. That's fine with me. I prefer the direct approach; it saves time. Chris and I have been lovers for the past eight months."

Stella's words flayed her, and the resulting pain brought tears to her eyes. Was she telling the truth? Had she and Christopher been having an affair? And if so, could Karyn hold him responsible since he'd forgotten his marriage? Yes, her heart answered bitterly, she would hold him responsible.

"Listen, dear," Stella continued in a condescending voice, "I hope you're not tiring him out. I know Chris is a fantastic lover, but he's not completely well yet, is he? I must confess that I find it highly suspicious that the only thing he forgot was you. You know that hysterical amnesia is a reflection of subconscious desires: a situation is so distasteful that you forget it, block it from your mind. That seems to be what your husband did. I've spent the past year with him, and I know for a fact that he didn't act like a married man, or at least a faithful married man! But then, you couldn't expect him to, could you, since he felt he was single? He certainly livened up Milwaukee."

"Is that why you dragged him up there?" Karyn burst out.

"You're getting hysterical, dear. Why don't you run home to Mama?" Stella's voice was saccharine sweet and laced with vindictiveness.

"Christopher loves me," Karyn insisted fiercely.

"If it pleases you to think that, go right ahead. You'll discover the error of your ways when I take what's rightfully mine right out from under you," she said crudely. "Chris may not love me at the moment," Stella freely admitted, "but he does want me, and I know how to play on his desires. Have you discovered how sensitive the scar on his hip is? We'll soon be lovers again; after all, we've only been apart a few weeks. I'll take Chris all right, or make him take me. I remember the time we made love in front of the fire . . ."

Karyn slammed the phone down, wishing she could stop the flow of pain as effectively as she had stopped Stella's venomous flow of words. Should she confront Christopher and ask him exactly what his relationship had been with Stella? It was all too sordid for words. And could she really believe him if he denied it? Christopher could well lie to save her pain, to save their marriage. Where now was all her romantic optimism of this morning?

The agonizing dilemma was unwittingly solved by Christopher later that evening. "I may have some encouraging news."

"You remembered something?"

"No," he replied rather abruptly. "I meant about Stella."

"Stella?" Fear choked her voice.

"Yes, I think she and Bob Martin may be making a go of it."

Karyn exhaled her pent-up breath. "Why is that encouraging?"

"Because I'd like to see her as happily married as I am. After all, I do owe her a great deal. She helped me a lot those first months."

"Only the first months?"

"Well, I haven't seen much of her since I've moved to Chicago. My way of dealing with the amnesia was to immerse myself in my work until I didn't have the time or the energy for anything else. After several months at that pace my doctor ordered me to take a break, so I went to Bermuda."

Figuring the time span, that meant there was no way Stella and Christopher could've been having an affair. Relief seeped through her like a balm. Karyn should've guessed. Stella was a pro at the devious art of lying. Look at what she'd done to Christopher. Telling him he lived in Milwaukee was a blatant fabrication. The other woman had gambled on Karyn's inability to confront her husband with her suspicions. She'd never dreamt that Christopher himself would bring up the topic of his own accord, ignorant of Stella's malicious lies.

"Hey, what are you looking so happy about?" he teased.

Her lingering kiss was answer enough.

Unfortunately, the problem of Stella didn't disappear, because the other woman simply refused to give up. She made waves whenever she could, and her position as Christopher's temporary secretary granted her ample opportunity. The offensive campaign against Karyn's marriage continued throughout the next week as Christopher was late coming home from work three nights out of five. Stella's explanatory calls were always made late enough to insure that dinner was ruined and she had to give her husband's portion to the racoons that roamed the woods in back of the house.

After the third such ruined evening, Friday night, Karyn decided that she would confront Christopher about the matter. He got home just before 9:00 P.M.

"I'd like to talk to you," she said.

He flopped down next to her and sprawled full-length on the couch, wearily resting his head on the soft cushion of her lap. Her fingers combed through the lock of hair that fell across his forehead. He looked so tired that she didn't have the heart to bring up Stella's name straightaway.

"How are the negotiations going?" she asked, remembering what he had told her about the reason for his overtime.

"Slowly," Christopher muttered in disgust. "We were just given another pile of forms to fill out, without which we can't continue any further. I can't believe all the red tape involved in getting this contract; the government regulations are ridiculous. I've filled out five different forms requesting the same information, because they have to go to five different departments. You'd think they could all use the same form, but no, that would be too simple. We have to keep all the bureaucrats busy!"

Unable to keep it bottled up any longer, Karyn spoke out. "Would you please have Stella call me earlier if you're going to be late? I've had to give your dinner to the racoons every night you were late this week, and although I'm sure they appreciate it, I really would rather not cook for the local wildlife!"

"Stella's still getting used to office procedures," he excused her. "We've really been busy, and I suppose it just skips her mind until close to normal quitting time."

Karyn jumped on his words. "That's just it. Stella's not used to office procedure, but I am. I'm a fully trained secretary, and I can come in with you to help at the office

131

until you can hire someone." Her excitement grew as she warmed to her theme. "I'm sure you'd get the work done a lot faster with someone experienced in this line of work assisting you."

"Honey, I can't just fire Stella like that after she's been helping me all week. Besides, you would be much too distracting. I wouldn't get any work done with you around," he kidded.

"Why do you always take her side instead of mine?" Karyn's voice reflected her jealous resentment.

Christopher lifted his head in surprise, then sat up, wincing slightly as he did so.

"It's not a matter of sides—this isn't a war. You're my wife and I love you; Stella is a friend who is helping me out of a jam."

"You're saying that you prefer to spend the day with her in the office rather than me," Karyn accused, "even though I'm much better qualified to help you."

"That's not the case at all," he said stiffly. "You appear to have the mistaken idea that you and Stella are competing for something. I don't know where you got a notion like that, but I really think you should work on this insecurity of yours instead of trying to put the blame on other people. Now, I'm tired, and I'm going to bed." With that he left the room.

Karyn sat on the couch for some time afterwards, the tears slowly running down her cheeks. This was the first time Christopher had been deliberately unkind to her, and it uncoiled a painful knot of fear. The gross inequity of it all scraped on her frayed nerves and made her cry even more. Stella seemed to hold all the cards. How could she hope to fight back? Karyn was no good at the back-stabbing games that Stella took pleasure in.

Wiping away her tears with the back of her hand, she vowed that she would talk to Christopher's doctor to find out how much of the truth he could be told. She didn't think she could continue this way, unable to defend herself for fear of upsetting him. Slowly making her way up to their bedroom much later, she found her husband asleep, his back facing her. She didn't have the courage to try and break through the defenses he had raised.

She slept very little that night, waking late the next morning to find the place beside her empty, which surprised her because Christopher usually told her when he was leaving. Putting on her cotton robe she went downstairs, but he was nowhere in sight. She anxiously went to the garage door and was relieved to find that his car was still there, so he couldn't be far away. After going back upstairs and quickly dressing, she went outside to see if he was working in the yard. She found him way at the back of the lot, clearing away some debris that had gotten caught in the undergrowth.

"Good morning," she greeted him quietly. "Did you eat breakfast?"

"No."

"Oh. I'll go make something then. French toast all right?"

"Fine."

She returned to the house, unable to gauge his mood from his short answers. The egg-coated bread was sizzling in the pan when Christopher walked up behind her. Planting a kiss on the nape of her neck, he reached around to present her with a bouquet of flowers from the garden.

"Thank you," she murmured after smelling the lovely array that included several deep-purple irises. She lowered the flame on the stove before going to put the flowers in a vase, which she placed on the small table in the breakfast nook. After breakfast, sensing that his mood was more receptive, she asked him, "Would you humor me by doing something?"

"Depends on what it is," he answered warily.

Karyn sighed. Christopher never used to be so cautious.

133

"Please don't leave me in the morning without waking me up and telling me where you're going. Otherwise I worry about you."

"There's no cause to worry," she was sharply informed.

"It's a small thing to ask."

"All right," he grudgingly agreed.

While helping her stack the dirty dishes in the dishwasher he informed her, "I got an appointment for you with Dr. Schneider," naming the doctor who had treated him for his amnesia.

And so it was that she found herself in Dr. Schneider's office on Tuesday morning.

"I want to thank you for taking the time to see me, Dr. Schneider," Karyn said.

"Not at all," the distinguished-looking, gray-haired doctor assured her. "So, Mr. Reid is married. Has this discovery prompted any memory recall?"

Karyn explained the details of their meeting in Bermuda, Christopher's eventual recognition, and his continued blankness about the night of his disappearance.

"I imagine you've got a lot of questions," the doctor shrewdly guessed. "Please feel free to ask."

"Do you have any idea what's causing his amnesia?"

"We did a series of thorough tests after your husband's accident. There was no organic or physical reason for his amnesia. Cases like these are therefore called hysterical amnesia. Mr. Reid is suffering from retrograde hysterical amnesia, where events directly preceding the causative event are forgotten. These memories are not actually lost," Dr. Schneider went on to assure her. "They are simply pushed to a recess of the mind that temporarily can't be reached."

Karyn blushed painfully before asking the question that had been foremost in her mind.

"Do you know why he remembered everything else except me?"

134

"You said there were no misunderstandings or emotional strain between the two of you prior to his disappearance?"

"That's right."

"Well, it's not unusual in cases like this for the long-term amnesia to relate only to particular memories. We are generally quite pleased with the way your husband has been recovering . . . picking up the threads of his new life in Chicago. Of course, he hadn't run into anyone who knew him before the accident, other than Stella Dukane, that is. I presume you've met her?"

"Yes, I have. Dr. Schneider, Christopher has said that Stella told him he was living in Milwaukee before the accident."

"That's correct," the doctor agreed.

"No, it's not!" Karyn denied gravely. "As I said earlier, Christopher disappeared on our wedding night. We had just flown in from Lincoln, Nebraska, where he'd been working on his master's degree since graduating in June from Oxford University in England. He's *never* lived in Milwaukee!"

The doctor looked startled. "Are you insinuating that Ms. Dukane deliberately lied to your husband?"

"I'm not insinuating it. I'm stating it as a fact," she asserted emphatically.

"You haven't told your husband, have you?"

"No, I wanted to check with you first."

"Good, I'm glad you did. As I said earlier, I'm pleased with your husband's recovery. These things can't be rushed. I don't want him exposed to any undue emotional stress right now, and I'm afraid your disclosure would cause a great deal of that."

"Do you have any suggestions as to what might help him fill in the remaining gaps?"

"Sometimes hypnosis is successful. Even more extreme would be another physical shock. But I don't want to hit

135

Mr. Reid over the head with a baseball bat in the hope of getting him to remember! I would prefer the process to be done naturally when his system is ready to accept it."

Karyn left the doctor's office feeling very frustrated. She'd asked the doctor all the questions that had been haunting her, but she'd left with fuzzy answers, no direct cure. The only definite thing was that Christopher was not to be exposed to any stress. In that regard Stella had been telling the truth—probably the only time she had, Karyn thought to herself bitterly.

Christopher walked in the front door later that evening to find his wife precariously perched upon a chair, apparently trying to fix a drooping section of the dining room drapes. He quickly strode over to her, his shoes silent on the thick plush carpet.

"What do you think you're doing?" he demanded.

Startled by the sound of his voice, she quickly turned around and felt herself slipping. When he tried to catch her, she catapulted into him with a force that knocked them both to the floor. Christopher bore the brunt of the fall, his body cushioning hers. Karyn quickly scrambled off him, anxiously searching his face, noting his closed eyes and pale features with dismay.

"Darling, are you all right?" she whispered tremulously.

He groaned before answering. "My God, you nearly killed me. You hit me like a ton of bricks."

Relieved that he was not seriously injured, she mockingly reproved him. "I can see the headlines now: INNOCENT HUSBAND SQUASHED BY FALLING WIFE. How romantic!"

"Romantic, eh?" His roguish blue eyes gleamed as he quirked his eyebrows. In one effortless movement he rolled over and captured her body with his, his warm mouth drifting over her face. Recalling the last time they were in this situation Karyn reminded him, "There's no fire now!"

His fingers stroked and rubbed the secret hollows of her body, arousing her as only he could, while his lips played games with hers.

"Yes, there is. Can't you feel it?" Christopher murmured hoarsely. The flames licked her body as she nodded and urged him closer, letting the warmth of his passion engulf her.

CHAPTER NINE

The next few weeks found Karyn settling down into a new routine. It was a change for her to spend all day at home after being accustomed to working. Actually, she still seemed to spend the day working. Only at home rather than in an office, she thought to herself as she unplugged the vacuum cleaner in the living room.

The weather had been warm, but not uncomfortably so. On this morning the sunshine beckoned her to desert the vacuum and come outside to frolic. Using the excuse of mailing some letters, Karyn escaped into the bright outdoors. It was about time for a break anyway, she thought, noting the magic hour of ten and recalling some of her fellow employees back in Seattle to whom the fifteen-minute coffee break was sacred.

The nearest mailbox was only a few blocks away, and she enjoyed strolling down the tree-lined streets, looking at the neighborhood. There was a nice sampling of all types and ages of houses in the area. Karyn was admiring the gingerbread ornateness of one of the older homes when someone coming at a fast clip around the corner nearly ran into her.

"Oh, I'm sorry!" a petite woman in her thirties huffed. "I was concentrating on keeping my strides even and didn't see you. Are you new around here?" she asked with friendly curiosity.

"Yes, I'm Karyn Reid."

"Oh, so you're Christopher's new wife! We've all been very curious about you. Gee, here I am going on, and I haven't introduced myself. I'm Marie Ames. I live right across the street from you, in the red and white house."

"Have you been jogging long?" Karyn inquired.

"No, this is only my third day, and it's getting harder each time instead of easier. Maybe I'm not cut out to be in the next Olympics!" she kidded. "Do you jog?"

"No, I could never warm up to the idea."

"Umm, I'm beginning to agree with you. Actually, it's probably not very practical in this climate. I mean, if I don't drop dead from heat prostration running around in the fierce heat of July, I'll probably be frozen to death in the sub-zero temperatures of winter. All right, I give up—you've talked me out of jogging!" She laughed at Karyn's concerned features. "That's okay; I had to have someone to blame my laziness on, and you just happened to be handy. I've been looking for an excuse to quit since about five minutes after I started!" Marie confessed.

Karyn knew she was going to enjoy having Marie live so near. She had a warm and honest character that seeded good friendship. They walked back to Marie's house, where she asked Karyn to join her for some coffee and cake. The comfortable ranch-style house was nicely furnished. Although the furniture wasn't new or stylish, it had a feeling of truly being lived in—no vinyl covers protecting everything from harm. This house was meant to be enjoyed and it was.

Marie waited until they were sitting at the table in the kitchen before inviting, "Tell me about yourself."

"I was born and bred in Lincoln, Nebraska, and I've been working the past year or so in Seattle. There's not much more than that."

"There's a lot more than that," Marie protested. "Like how you caught the most eligible bachelor in the neighborhood. He goes on vacation in Bermuda—we knew because

139

he asked us to keep an eye on the house while he was gone—and he comes back two weeks later announcing he got married. Two weeks after that you show up. Tell me if I'm prying, but I am interested."

Karyn recited the agreed-upon story. "Christopher and I had met before running into each other in Bermuda. We were in love, so we got married."

"Was it hard getting married abroad? I mean, Bermuda's not an American territory is it?"

Lord, she and Christopher hadn't thought of that question popping up. She'd better think fast.

"Actually, I knew someone in the government who was able to smooth the way, and we didn't have much trouble." The excuse sounded weak to her, but Marie bought it.

"You make it sound so commonplace, but I'll bet it was real romantic."

"We both enjoyed it," Karyn admitted shyly.

"What kind of work did you do in Seattle?"

"I was a legal secretary. Now it's your turn. Tell me about yourself," Karyn prompted.

"My husband, Jerry, and I have been living here for seven years. We've got two children: Amy is two and Tommy is seven. Tommy's in first grade and Amy is at my mother's for the day. All in all, I sound like a normal American housewife."

"No, I object to that."

"What, to my being normal?" Marie questioned with mock huffiness.

Karyn laughed. "No, to your being a housewife. You're married to a man, not a house. You are a typical American homemaker."

"Are you trying to raise my consciousness as a member of the feminist movement?"

"I don't look at it that way. I feel that you should be given credit for what you do. I know that as a legal secretary, I would often do things that were above and beyond what would be expected for that position, and before I quit I was trying to get the title raised to a legal assistant, because it more aptly described the work done. Now, don't you think that homemaker more aptly describes the work you do?"

"Yes, it does. I can tell we're going to have an interesting time with you around. Already I've quit jogging and taken up homemaking all in one afternoon!" Marie laughed.

Karyn spent several enjoyable hours with Marie and by the time Christopher came home that evening, she was eagerly waiting to tell him about her new friend. He dropped a quick kiss on her lips before going to wash up for dinner. When he came back into the kitchen, she told him about her day.

"I met Marie Ames today. She lives across the street."

"Ummm, this smells good," Christopher noted appreciatively, sniffing the spaghetti sauce. Dipping a finger in the cooling pot, he added, "Tastes good, too. Here," he dipped his finger in again and held it up to her mouth, "try it." She did so, nipping his finger before releasing it.

"Hey!" he cried in surprise. "What was that for?"

"You weren't listening to what I was saying."

"Sure I was. You said you met Marie Ames today. I'm glad you two are finally getting acquainted. She's 'nice people.' "

"Yes, she is," Karyn agreed, pausing to hand him a bowl of salad with salad tongs. "Would you put that on the table, please? Then I think we're ready to eat."

She brought in the spaghetti, and they sat down at the dining room table, facing the garden and woods at the back of the house.

"Marie is nice," she continued. "That's why I felt so bad lying to her."

"Lying to her?" he asked.

141

"Yes, about how we met in Bermuda and got married. In fact, she asked me if we had trouble doing so in a foreign country."

"I never thought of that. What did you say?"

"I made some feeble excuse about knowing someone in the government who smoothed the way for us. It really goes against the grain for me to lie like that."

"I know it does," he said sympathetically. "But do you think telling the truth would have been any easier?"

"No, I have to agree with you there," she admitted. "It would have been horrendous to try and explain everything, and it really isn't anyone else's business. Not that Marie was trying to pry," she hurriedly went on. "She was just curious to . . . umm, now how did she put it?" Karyn bit her lip in mock concentration. "Oh, yes, Marie was curious to know how I caught the most eligible bachelor in the neighborhood!"

Christopher laughed, his white teeth gleaming in his tanned face. "I don't know that that's such a great compliment. I'm the only bachelor in the area besides a crusty old widower in his sixties a block away!"

Karyn joined in his laughter, and the conversation swung to his job as the dinner progressed.

"I've put an ad in the paper for a new secretary: it should be running this weekend. That means I'll start interviewing applicants the week after next."

She was relieved to hear that plans to hire a permanent secretary were being implemented. It couldn't happen soon enough for her. Stella's harassing phone calls were beginning to take a toll. Karyn had trouble sleeping, disturbed by vivid nightmares of Christopher walking away with Stella. These lurking fears tugged painfully at her heart, but she masked her apprehension well.

After dinner Karyn put the dirty dishes in the dishwasher and turned it on before going to join her husband

142

in the living room where they planned on watching a program on public television.

He wasn't in the room, so she went over and turned on the set, adjusting it to get the best picture. Since there were a few minutes left before the show began, Karyn settled down on the couch and sorted through the junk mail that had come earlier in the day.

She heard Christopher call down from the top of the stairs. "Could you come up here for a minute? I've got something to show you."

"Sure, just a second." She threw away three letters addressed to "occupant" and made her way upstairs. He met her outside their bedroom door, which was closed.

"Give me your hand, and close your eyes."

"What is this?" she laughed.

"Do what I ask and you'll find out."

When she closed her eyes, he took hold of her hand and gently drew her into the bedroom. "Now keep them closed," he ordered, urging her over to the bed.

"Darling, the special is going to be on in a few minutes, and I really don't think we'll have time to . . ." Karyn broke off as she felt a carton the size of a shoe box placed in her hands.

"What on earth!" she began, but he interrupted her with, "You can open your eyes now."

She did so to find a beautiful, gray Persian kitten curled up in the cardboard box, looking up at her with drowsy blue eyes.

"She's gorgeous!" Karyn exclaimed, sitting on the bed and scooping the kitten out of the box and onto her lap. "Whose is she?"

"How did you know it was a she?" Christopher asked dryly, sitting down next to her.

"Instinct," was her pert reply.

"Then instinct should also have told you that this female kitten is yours. I know how you love cats and have

143

always wanted one, but with your mother's allergies and the landlord's ruling of 'no pets' you never had the chance."

"Darling, you remembered that! What a great sign. You see, you are remembering more and more each day," she congratulated him enthusiastically.

He looked surprised. "I never even thought about it. I just knew about your love of cats, and the rest followed naturally."

"That's the way the remainder of the blankness will be filled in until you know the whole story. But thank you for the kitten. I really love her."

"Do I have a rival for your attention now?" he teased.

The kitten scrambled off her lap and began investigating the rest of the bed, jumping at imaginary lumps under the bedcover. Karyn turned and pushed her husband back onto the bed. Leaning over him she crooned, "Poor baby, are you jealous? I still love you," softly stroking his lower lip with her finger. He grabbed the arm she was resting on, and without its support Karyn collapsed onto his chest.

"I've got you now," he growled. "What are you going to do about it?"

"Enjoy it!" she promptly retorted. Lowering her mouth to his, she bestowed a warm kiss before they were interrupted by the kitten who had decided to climb up Christopher's pant leg and join Karyn on his chest. Once there, the kitten began to play with the ends of Karyn's hair as its curtain of softness swung across his shirt.

"See," she laughed. "The kitten loves you too!" Karyn picked up the little gray ball of fluffy fur, and they went back downstairs to watch the special.

"Do you have some food for her?"

"Yes, I gave her some upstairs and there is also a kitty litter box. I was assured that she is housebroken."

Karyn decided to keep a close eye on the kitten until it was proved that that was the case!

144

"What are you going to name her?" he asked.

She watched the kitten sniffing around the bottom of the chair before going on to investigate the next obstacle. "I'm going to name her Mouse," she decided.

"You're going to name your cat Mouse?" Christopher repeated incredulously. "You'll give her an identity crisis," he warned.

"I don't think so. Look. 'Here, Mouse, come here,' " and sure enough, the little kitten's ears perked, and she turned her head to look at Karyn.

"See!" she said triumphantly. "She knows her name!"

Mouse soon tired of the expedition around the living room and decided to jump up and join them on the couch. She curled up on Karyn's lap, while Karyn curled up on Christopher's lap. They both enjoyed the program and the companionship they shared that evening.

Sometime during the short intermission Christopher moved his hand inside the collar of Karyn's shirt to rest it on the smooth bare curve of her shoulder. She enjoyed having him touch her just for touching's sake. Basking in the warmth of his love, she trustingly lay against him. Their love was not a passionate explosion that soon died out, she fancifully thought to herself; it was more like an eternal flame that burned constantly in their hearts. Not that their relationship lacked passionate explosions, but underneath there was more.

The theme music at the end of the program was interrupted by the ringing of the phone on the adjoining table. Christopher answered it.

"Hello? Yes, she is. Is this Mrs. Kadik? This is Christopher. How are you? That's good. Here's Karyn," and he handed her the receiver.

"Hello, Mother."

"Oh, thank God you're all right," her mother sighed in relief.

"All right?" she questioned blankly. "Why wouldn't I be all right?"

"Well, Christopher is suffering from some kind of mental problem."

"We've already talked about that, Mother. How are you and Dad?"

"Oh, we're fine. We won the bridge tournament last night."

"That's great. Congratulations! You must be proud of yourselves."

"Yes, we're going to have a party at Lucy's house. You know," her voice lowered confidentially, "her son . . ." Mrs. Kadik went on for several minutes with the latest gossip about her friends.

"Just a moment. Your father would like to talk to you. It's Karyn, dear," she explained to her absentminded husband.

"Hello, Karyn. Everything all right up there?"

"Yes, it's fine, Dad." They talked for a while before she said, "Christopher would like to speak to you for a moment"—this in answer to her husband's waving hands and pantomimic motions. He took the phone.

"Mr. Kadik, I just wanted to assure you and your wife that I intend to take very good care of your daughter. She won't lack for anything, sir. I can promise you that," he stated earnestly.

There was a momentary silence that was broken by Christopher's laughter at her father's response. "Good night, sir."

After he'd hung up, she demanded, "What did he say?"

"He said in a very puzzled voice that you've never lacked anything before, so why should he worry about that now? I hope he didn't think I was insinuating that you were underfed or anything! And speaking of food, how would you feel about having some kind of get-together for the people at work?"

"What kind of get-together, and for how many?"

He shrugged. "About twenty-five people for a barbecue outside, weather permitting."

"I suppose I'll have to meet them sometime," Karyn sighed. "When?"

"When would be good for you?"

"How about two weeks from next Saturday?"

"That would be the seventeenth. Yes, that sounds good."

"Christopher, I've never done anything like this before. Do we send out invitations or what?"

"I suppose that would be a good idea. Why don't you pick some up, and I'll hand them out to the people at work."

"Can I invite Marie and Jerry Ames?"

"You can invite whoever you want."

"They're the only people I know in this area. Marie might have some pointers for me."

The two intervening weeks rushed past in a hubbub of activity, with Karyn thoroughly cleaning the house from top to bottom, rearranging furniture, and checking cookbooks for hors d'oeuvres, among other things. The invitations had been duly dispatched, and so far, everyone had responded favorably. She hadn't been able to prevent Christopher from inviting Stella and was reluctant to make a fuss about it in view of Dr. Schneider's cautionary words. The day Stella received her invitation she called Karyn, supposedly to offer her assistance, but actually to stir up trouble.

"I'm really looking forward to this barbecue." The enthusiasm in Stella's voice immediately made Karyn suspicious. "Are you sure you don't need my help?"

"Positive," Karyn firmly replied, preferring to depend on the solid reliability of Marie's assistance.

"Chris's friends will be surprised to meet you. You're not exactly his type."

"I am his wife," Karyn pointed out.

"For the time being. It won't last long. The appeal of a simpering virgin will soon wane. Chris needs an experienced woman, not an inept novice. He's a sexy man; I get turned on just listening to him speak in that smooth voice of his."

"Well, turn yourself off, because he's mine. You've got one hell of a nerve talking like that about my husband!"

"Your tiny mind is too preoccupied with social niceties. Much as I'd like to, I don't have the time to list all your faults. See you at the party!"

To Karyn, Stella's promise sounded more like a threat. Where's your backbone? she rallied herself. Don't let Stella push you around. Wear something fabulous to the party —something that'll knock their eyes out.

Karyn put almost as much thought into choosing her outfit as she did planning the entire barbecue. Skirts, pants, and tops covering an entire spectrum of colors were piled on the bed, as she would try on one combination and then shake her head and take it off, putting it on the reject pile. This took up the better part of the Friday afternoon before the party. She was getting near the end of her patience, believing, or fearing, that she would never find anything acceptable to wear, when she found the winning combination of a boldly patterned full skirt in shades of purples, blues, and white and a matching purple cotton shirt with short raglan sleeves and a V neck.

That was the last barricade hurtled, she sighed to herself. Now there was only the party to live through. And she had to confess that she did rather dread the coming evening, the main reason being Stella's appearance. Karyn was going to feel nervous enough meeting Christopher's working associates, without having Stella's contemptuous eyes watching over everything, ready to spot and gloat over the slightest mistake.

Time couldn't be halted and the night of the party was

soon upon her. The local meteorologist promised a beautiful evening. Although it had been quite warm during the day, the temperature had dropped to a comfortable 72°F.

She was pleased with her appearance: the outfit she'd chosen the day before still looked good to her. Her morale had gotten a boost when Christopher had walked in while she was putting the finishing touches to her hair, plaited into a twist on the side of her head. His indigo eyes warmly appraised her, and his mouth formed a silent whistle of appreciation.

"You look gorgeous," he proclaimed. "Every man there tonight is going to be jealous of me. I hope no one tries to stab me in the back," he joked, before turning pale as conflicting emotions played over his face.

"Honey, what is it?"

He put both hands to his head, palms pressed to his temples with eyes closed as if in fierce concentration. "There it is again, that feeling of some kind of memory being just out of reach. Now it's gone. Damn it!" he exclaimed in savage frustration. "Why can't I remember and have done with it?"

Karyn could feel the waves of his self-deprecating anger, could see the strain etched on his face. She slid her arms around him, feeling the tenseness slowly leave his body as she held him in her arms, pouring out all the love she felt for him. They stood there for a timeless moment.

"Thanks," he said huskily, easing her out of his embrace to examine her face. "The closer you are, the better you look."

Karyn smiled her appreciation. "What jewelry do you think I should wear tonight?" wanting to drag his thoughts away from their present unhappy direction.

"How about the purple shell necklace from Bermuda?"

She pulled the necklace out of her jewelry case, where it had been safely tucked away in the box from the store. "I suppose you've been good, so I'll trust you to put it on

149

for me," she graciously decided, then ruined the effect of haughty disdain by giggling when he blew in her ear. "No fair! You know I'm ticklish there."

"I always tease impudent wives," she was informed. "Now stop squirming, or we'll be up here all night; and while that does sound extremely enjoyable, it would be rather embarrassing for our guests!"

Christopher soon had the small fastening clasped and turned her around. "Right, now for your appreciation."

"You're sure getting your money's worth out of this necklace," Karyn murmured, reaching up to rub her mouth across his until his lips caught hers in a deeply satisfying kiss. Sheer liquid fire ran through her veins, and her toes curled into the large oriental rug that now decorated their bedroom floor.

Removing his warm lips ever so slightly, Christopher whispered, "Thank you."

"Ummm?" she murmured, unable to resist the temptation of resting her lips against his when they were this close.

"For not being the kind of person who won't let you touch her for fear of messing up her makeup."

"I've learned not to put much on with you around!"

He laughed but was prevented from taking action at her provocative statement by the sound of the doorbell. Glancing at the clock on their nightstand, he remarked, "Someone's early."

He left the room to answer the persistent ringing, while Karyn stopped a moment to reapply her lipstick before following him. She came downstairs to find Stella gazing at her husband with a hungry, predatory look in her eyes.

"Chris, you've got lipstick smeared all over." Stella reached into her clutch to pull out a small handkerchief. She rested one hand on Christopher's arm, while the other possessively and meticulously rubbed his lips, as if to rub off Karyn's claim on him as well as her kiss.

150

"Hey, not so hard!" Christopher protested.

"I'd kiss it better, but I wouldn't want Karyn to get the wrong idea. Do stop hovering there on the stairs and join us," Stella condescendingly instructed her in a purring voice.

Karyn felt the blood rush to her cheeks, both in anger and embarrassment. Just who did Stella think she was, giving out orders like that! This wasn't her house, and Christopher wasn't her husband. Stick up for your rights, she silently goaded.

"I wasn't hovering," Karyn corrected. "Just waiting for the performance to end." There, put that in your pipe and smoke it, she thought to herself triumphantly. She could tell by the gleam in Stella's cold eyes that she would be made to pay for that comment later in the evening.

"I came early because I thought you might need some help, this being your first party and all. I don't imagine you've done much entertaining, and while the guests are only friends from the office, I think first impressions are so important, don't you?"

And I'm going to make sure yours are awful, Stella's look silently continued.

"Thank you, but I really don't need any help. Marie should be here in a few minutes, and everything seems to be under control."

"Well then, you won't mind if I steal your husband for a minute. Chris, I wanted to ask you about that file you gave me today," Stella began, urging him over to the couch in the living room and sitting down almost on top of him.

Karyn stomped into the kitchen where she found Mouse sitting in front of her dish in an explicitly demanding pose for an early dinner.

"I'd better give you your food upstairs, so you don't sneak out when any of the guests are here," she told the kitten before bending down to pick her up. But the precocious kitten decided that if she couldn't get dinner now, she might as well enjoy a game of chase and raced off toward the living room with Karyn following at a slightly slower pace.

"Oh, what have we got here!" Stella exclaimed. "I just adore cats. Isn't it sweet. What's its name?" she asked Christopher.

"Mouse," he answered, trying to keep a straight face.

"No, the cat's name."

"That's right—the cat's name is Mouse."

"Let me guess, Karyn thought of that, didn't she? A bit of adolescent humor. How clever," Stella drawled. When the kitten came closer to sniff the stranger, Stella bent down to pet her, hiding her disgust as she did so. She hated cats and always had: they were so quiet, slinking around and sneaking up on people without any warning. However, if Chris had one he must like them, so it wouldn't hurt to make a show of affection.

Cats are very sensitive to vibrations, though, and Mouse sensed the hatred emitting from this stranger like the foul smell emitting from her kitty litter box when it was dirty. If cat haters ignore a cat, it will fawn all over them just to prove a point. But if they pretend a liking they don't feel, the cat will show its dislike much much more openly.

So, as Stella reached down to pet Mouse, the little kitten's fur stood on end, and she fluffed herself out to twice her normal size, for effect, before spitting and hissing, causing Stella to inelegantly jump back in fright. Before Stella could retaliate by kicking the kitten, Karyn had scooped it up into her arms out of harm's way, where Mouse began to purr contentedly.

"I don't know what's wrong with her. She's usually very friendly. Maybe she's hungry," Karyn excused the kitten. "I was just taking her upstairs to give her dinner in our room and then lock her in so she wouldn't get underfoot during the party."

"She seems a vicious animal to me," Stella spat. "If I didn't love animals so much I would suggest that you have it put down." At Christopher's start of surprise she recalled herself and continued on a calmer note. "Luckily, I know that if cats are spoiled, they can resort to hostile behavior."

Carrying the purring bundle of fur upstairs, Karyn regretted Mouse's bad behavior but could understand it, because she'd felt like spitting and hissing at Stella too!

She left Mouse with a full dish of food and water, along with the required kitty litter box, then descended the stairs for the second time that evening to find Stella hanging onto Christopher's arm and welcoming the new arrivals. Her throat constricted painfully as she observed how perfectly at home Stella seemed, her confidence and self-assurance leading one to believe she was his new wife instead of Karyn. She didn't know where she would've gotten the courage to continue her solitary descent if Marie hadn't caught sight of her and come right over.

"You look fantastic. I'm green with envy. You can carry off those exotic-looking outfits with your coloring. This thing looks like a rag in comparison," she kidded, looking down at her own attractive red- and white-striped sun dress.

That kind of bantering was exactly what Karyn's sagging self-confidence needed. She smiled gratefully and came down the rest of the stairs. "Marie, you look great. Where's Jerry?"

"Christopher's got him tending the bar. It didn't take much arm-twisting—I think he always had this fantasy of being a bartender."

"Do you know any of the people here?" she asked Marie nervously.

"You mean you haven't been introduced yet?" her new friend demanded incredulously. "What can your husband be thinking of?"

Hearing Stella's tinkling laughter over the low murmur of Christopher's voice, Karyn thought the answer to that question was obvious. A tall, stockily built man interrupted her jealous speculations. "You must be Karyn," he said in a deep, gravelly voice. Putting out a large hand, he introduced himself. "I'm Bob Martin. I don't know if Chris has talked about me?"

Karyn hastily composed herself, unable to avoid responding to the man's unassuming friendliness. "Yes, he has told me about you, Mr. Martin."

Shaking her outstretched hand, he invited her, "Call me Bob, please. It was rather a shock when Chris came back from vacation and announced he was married, but now that I've met you I can understand perfectly."

She found herself blushing at his gallantry. "Thank you."

"Now Bob, don't go flirting with her; she's a respectable married woman," Marie teased.

"Marie, how good to see you. How are the kids?"

Karyn looked from one to the other in surprise. "You've met?"

"Yes, Marie and her husband were over several times when Chris had us come for dinner."

"I was going to tell you that Bob is the only guest I'd met before, with the exception of Stella, of course."

Of course, Karyn thought to herself bitterly. Jealousy rose in her throat, swamping her mind and consuming her thoughts. She was threading her way toward the dining room when Christopher caught sight of her shimmering auburn hair above the crowd. He quickly disengaged himself from Stella's clinging fingers, and offering his excuses to the group gathered around them, made his way over to her.

"Darling, where have you been?"

"Right here. You can't have been looking very hard for me," she retorted bitterly.

"Come meet some of our guests." Grabbing hold of her hand, he pulled her toward the group he had just left.

The names and faces of the people tended to get blurry after several rounds of introductions had been made. Everyone seemed to be enjoying themselves, except for the hostess. Christopher had been waylaid by Stella again, and Karyn was stuck in a corner listening to the rise and fall of conversation around her. Marie was talking with Bob and two other men and a woman out on the patio. She really had been a tremendous help during the evening.

It wasn't her friend's fault that the party was turning into a personal endurance test; the blame was entirely on Stella. She'd manipulated the entire evening so that Karyn rarely had time to be with her husband. Although Christopher had made up for his earlier inattentiveness by introducing her to most of the guests, he hadn't had time to complete the rounds before he was needed elsewhere to stop an argument about computer billing, or so Stella said.

When Karyn wandered away from the group she had been in, they didn't even stop their conversation, strengthening her feeling that she was an invisible outsider. She didn't know anything about computers so was unable to participate in the conversations going on with the men on one side of the room. On the other hand, she wasn't familiar with the names that the women were bandying about.

She ended up passing hors d'oeuvres around and had one poor man who had too much to drink ask if she was the caterer. Obviously, he was one of the guests Christopher hadn't gotten around to introducing her to. The woman next to him pointed out his error, and Karyn accepted his blundering apology before hurrying back to the kitchen, only to find groups of people collected there, too. She ended up spending the rest of the evening out on the patio with Marie, Jerry, Bob, and a pleasant couple called the Engletons. Christopher didn't join her until the guests began making their departures. Most thanked her for a lovely evening or complimented her on the food, especially her recipe for barbecued ribs. There were only four people left when Karyn wearily made her way upstairs.

She was shocked to see the closed door to their bedroom standing wide open, the 'Do Not Disturb' sign obviously ignored. Stella was nonchalantly wandering around the room, examining the contents of the dressing table as if she owned the place. Karyn felt unadulterated fury race through her body at the other woman's insolence.

"How dare you come in here!" Her voice was shaking with anger.

"You mean the 'Do Not Disturb' sign?" Stella asked innocently. "I knew that didn't apply to me. After all, I'm no stranger to this room; I helped Chris decorate it. By the way, I found a painting the other day that would be perfect up on that wall."

"He doesn't need your help anymore, Stella. This is my home, and I'm his wife." Karyn suddenly remembered the main reason for keeping the door shut in the first place—Mouse.

"Where's Mouse," she demanded in panic.

"Mouse?"

"The cat. I left her locked up here so she wouldn't get loose downstairs."

"Oh, she ran out of the room as soon as I opened the door."

"When was that?"

"About fifteen minutes ago."

Karyn abandoned the fight with Stella and raced downstairs calling the kitten. The sliding glass door was open, and the darkness seemed to beckon mockingly. She was certain the kitten would have discovered the escape route and grabbed at the opportunity to do some outdoor exploring.

"Karyn, what's the matter?" Christopher asked in concern.

"She let Mouse out," she accused bitterly before dashing through the open door. He ran after her, halting her with his hand on her arm.

"Calm down and tell me what you're talking about. Who let Mouse out?"

"Stella went upstairs and deliberately let Mouse out. She hates cats and wanted to get even with Mouse for spitting at her earlier."

Stella's voice wafted through the door. "Chris dear, I'm so sorry. I forgot which room was the washroom and mistakenly opened the door for just a minute, and the little thing rushed past me. You know I'd never do anything to hurt it. I expect Karyn is just upset from the worry. I know I would be, although I like to think that I wouldn't accuse others in the hope of making malicious trouble."

Karyn pulled away from her husband's restraining hand and ran out toward the woods. The full moon lit her way as she stumbled through the tangled undergrowth, scratching her legs and arms on sharp branches and thorny bushes along the way. Marie came out to see what the commotion was, and after Christopher explained that the kitten was missing, she and Jerry joined in the search, bringing flashlights to illuminate the woods. They softly called the kitten, not wanting to arouse the neighbors by yelling, but there was no answer. After about an hour of searching they wearily gave up for the night.

Marie tried to comfort Karyn before going home. "We had a cat once that got out and was gone for three days, but she came back. Cats are clever animals."

"We haven't had Mouse long enough for her to know where she lives. She won't be able to find her way back home," Karyn choked.

"Try to get some sleep. If she doesn't come back tonight, we'll look again in the morning."

157

Stella and Bob left with them, Stella unable to resist throwing one last gloating look over her shoulder before closing the door. Christopher came over and tried to calm her, but Karyn pulled away from him, unable to bear his touch right then. Her emotions were in a frenzy, and she was in no fit state to talk to him. After all, he had ignored her for most of the evening, treating her like an acquaintance rather than a wife.

"Honey, come up to bed. You can look again in the morning," he repeated Marie's advice.

"No, I'd rather sleep down here tonight. I'll leave the sliding door open in case she comes back."

"Then I'll stay with you," Christopher decided.

"No," she cried. "Just leave me alone! Please leave me alone!"

"All right," he said stiffly and went upstairs.

She didn't get much sleep that night, tossing restlessly in her makeshift bed on the living room couch. The bitter pain in her heart couldn't be eased. She felt a grave uncertainty about her ability to handle the continued strain of fighting Stella to save her marriage—if you could even call it a fight with Stella holding all the weapons and Karyn having her hands tied by the doctor's orders not to upset Christopher. Instead of helping, her visit with Dr. Schneider had only exacerbated the problem. Her inner doubts and fears continued to grow, yet she knew she couldn't reveal them to Christopher without running the risk of worsening his condition.

Tears of frustration filled her eyes. While life was becoming unbearable with him, she also knew that it would be unbearable without him, and therefore, found herself in a mental corner of being damned if she stayed and damned if she left. It was an untenable position, bound to wreak havoc on all concerned.

Burdened with anxiety, Karyn dozed intermittently, checking the patio every so often for a sign of the kitten.

She woke up very early in the morning to the pathetic sound of meowing. A very frightened Mouse was cowering outside. She slowly made her way over, careful not to make any sudden movements that might scare it. The little feline seemed to recognize her when she leaned down to pick it up.

"Oh Mousie, you had me so scared. You poor thing," she crooned to the trembling kitten in her arms.

Karyn brought her inside and closed the door. Taking a closer look, she saw that the kitten's long, fine fur was tangled with burs that she must have picked up in the woods. Some of them were obviously painful, so the first thing Karyn did was sit down and gently pull the irritating, sharp burs free from the fur. She ended up with three more scratches to match those she'd gotten in the woods last night, but Mouse was now as soft and smooth as when she'd left.

Karyn dropped her to the floor and went into the kitchen, where she softly called the kitten to come eat. A special reward of cream was poured into a small dish and set next to an already-full dinner dish. The kitten ate ravenously, but was still edgy, her blue eyes darting around the room while she ate.

Karyn made some coffee before sitting down at the breakfast nook, sympathizing with Mouse's agitation. The night's unrest hadn't brought her any nearer to a decision, except that things couldn't continue as they were. The problem was, she didn't know what to do to improve them.

CHAPTER TEN

Karyn was very cool when Christopher came down later that morning, blaming him for her disastrous night. For the first time since her arrival she was unable to feel at ease with him and spent the rest of the weekend by herself. Christopher tried to scale the wall she had built around herself but soon became frustrated by his failure to do so, and he in turn became remote.

This disturbing chain of events continued for several days and Christopher took to spending more time at his health club, where he attempted to relieve his frustrations in the rigors of handball. While the strenuous games tired him physically, they couldn't quiet the turbulent conflict churning within him. He became curt and irritable at work, reflecting the strain their disagreement was having on him.

The tension between them took its toll on Karyn as well, her animated features becoming pale and distracted as the days wore on. Marie noted the change in her friend with troubled eyes and offered a sympathetic ear. Karyn, however, was unable to confide in Marie without revealing the whole story about Christopher's disappearance. Her self-confidence drained away under the continued barrage of Stella's verbal barbs. The more withdrawn Christopher became, the more she wondered if he regretted finding her again. Demoralized by tormenting doubts, she retreated behind a wall of reserve. She was consumed with fear because he was drifting away from her, yet she was incapable of undertaking a move to make him stay.

This precarious state of affairs did not escape the eagle eye of Stella, who was waiting for precisely such an opportunity to make her move. Christopher was sitting at his desk, his shoulders hunched while he contemplated the pile of papers on his desk, absently rubbing his neck. Stella noted his action and made her move.

"Here, let me help," she replaced his hands with hers. "You're all tensed up; you should relax." Her trained massage soon began relieving the pain caused by the spastic muscles. "Is something bothering you? You know you can confide in me," her inviting voice grew softer.

He made no response but wearily leaned back. Stella gained confidence from his action, her eyes glittering in triumph. "You've been so tense since Karyn came back. Maybe this marriage isn't agreeing with you. That could have been the reason you forgot all about it—because it was too painful to remember."

Christopher had to admit that at this point in time, he wasn't certain about anything, except for the fact that he did love Karyn. Maybe that wasn't enough, and Stella was right . . . that he'd found out that this type of cold warfare was just too painful to continue.

Stella took his silence as a sign of agreement and came around from behind his chair to perch on its arm. "Love doesn't have to be this painful," she whispered seductively. "I know how to make you feel better, Chris darling— much better than she's ever made you feel," and she leaned over to kiss him, sinuously sliding onto his lap as she did so.

He was stunned by her behavior and pulled away in surprise.

"I love you," she said passionately, her lips feverishly trying to capture his. His hands grasped both of hers and removed them from their possessive hold before he pushed her off his lap.

"Stella, I never guessed you felt this way," he began awkwardly.

"Darling," she purred. "I knew you loved me."

"No, wait a minute. I really appreciate all the support you gave me after my accident, and I hate to have to hurt you like this . . ."

"Then don't," Stella interrupted, trying to pull him up into her arms. He stood up and walked over to the window.

"I love my wife."

"Karyn doesn't love you half as much as I do!" Stella's voice rose as she passionately stated her case. "If she had, she would've looked for you when you disappeared instead of moving as far away as she could."

"She did look for me," he protested vainly.

"Not very hard. But then, she isn't the kind of girl to really appreciate a man. You need a full-blooded, experienced woman, Chris—one who's not afraid to show her love for you," she continued shamelessly, "not some prude. She's no good for you."

Christopher's handsome face hardened ruthlessly as Stella's insults against Karyn grew more virulent and explicit. His eyes were cold chips of ice when he turned from the window to stride across the room, where he grabbed her shoulders and shook her to stop the bitter flow of words from her painted lips.

"Now, you listen to me," he instructed her harshly, "and you listen well. I love Karyn, and she loves me. As for being a prude, she has more sex appeal in her little finger than you have in your whole body. She doesn't have to advertise the fact to all and sundry. Your behavior here today has forfeited any claim you had on my friendship. You're fired, Stella. I want you out of my office right now. For Bob's sake, I won't mention this scene to him."

162

"Who gives a damn about Bob?" she shrieked. "It was you I wanted, only you were in such a haze that you didn't even know it. But then, disturbed people do that, don't they . . . wander around in a haze," Stella snarled. "And you are disturbed, Chris—there's no doubt of that."

Stella walked toward the office door, where she paused to turn and shoot one last venomous arrow.

"You're a crock. You haven't completely regained your memory after over a year, and my medical opinion is that you never will. You'll never be a normal, complete man again!" Her words scored a direct hit on his Achilles' heel.

Later that evening Karyn was preparing a julienne salad for dinner. The day had been oppressively hot and humid. She had changed into a cool pair of purple cotton shorts and a white camisole top because the jeans she had worn earlier in the day had proved to be much too warm. The thermostat on the air conditioner was turned up to conserve energy, for hopefully the night air would soon cool without the heat of the sun.

Her heart began to pound when she heard her husband's footsteps in the hall announcing his arrival home. Karyn had hashed the whole situation out today and had finally come to a decision: She was going to ask Christopher to fire Stella and hire a temporary secretary until he found someone suitable. In view of the doctor's advice Stella's past treachery and lies would not be brought up. She would simply ask him to do this for her.

Intent on her own announcement she only picked at her dinner. Succulent strips of chicken were chewed and swallowed without notice as she tried to work up enough nerve to broach the subject. His mood was impossible to gauge, although his tanned face did look weary, with lines of strain showing around his eyes and lips. He had loosened the tie he had worn to work and it hung limply down his blue shirt.

When he looked up, she hastily lowered her eyes. Taking a dinner roll and buttering it, he casually informed her, "By the way, I fired Stella today."

Karyn choked on the piece of lettuce she had just put in her mouth. "You what? Why?"

"Because she was trying to steal your husband. Did you know?"

"Yes, I knew. But when did you find out?"

"This afternoon."

Her unnatural restraint broke, and she jumped up out of her chair, rushing around the table to throw her arms around his neck and exclaim, "Oh, thank you! I was going to bring it up tonight, and I was so scared you'd think I was being unreasonable or paranoid or something." She fell laughing in relief onto his lap.

But her actions reminded him of the rest of the scene with Stella, and he gently pushed her off. "Go finish your dinner before it gets hot," he joked lamely.

This close to him she could see the etched lines of fatigue beside his mouth, the grim look in his normally quizzical eyes.

"Exactly what happened this afternoon?" she asked him quietly.

"Let's talk about it later. I've got a splitting headache and I'm hoping the food will ease it somewhat."

She swiftly resumed her seat and finished her dinner. Afterwards, she bade him to go into the living room and rest while she cleared up, then brought him some iced coffee and two aspirins. Christopher was very reluctant to talk about the scene in his office, and she had to pry the words out of him. She didn't want to appear insensitive, but she knew that it would be more damaging for him to keep whatever it was bottled up inside.

Gradually she was able to piece together the meeting with Stella. Although he had intended to omit her bitter accusations about his sanity and masculinity, Karyn gradually drew the truth out of him; she could imagine

164

how demanding Stella had become in her bid to possess him, his own anger at her actions, and her subsequent fury at defeat. Aware of the other woman's vicious nature, she knew the confrontation must've been extremely unpleasant.

She stood behind him while he talked, gently massaging the taut muscles of his neck and shoulders. Although she wasn't trained in that kind of therapy as Stella was, he found her hands to be more healing, because they were the hands he loved. She felt the strain in him gradually lessen as she tried to repair the damage Stella had inflicted.

"Stella was simply a woman scorned. Your memory will come back one day. Just be patient."

Christopher pulled one of her hands around to his mouth, where his tongue traced the pattern of veins across the sensitive skin of her wrist.

"As for you not being a complete man, you're more than man enough for me," she defended him vehemently. "And for Stella, too, or she would never have made a play for you in the first place!"

He exerted pressure on her arm, and keeping his lips on her wrist, he felt her pulse quicken in alarm when he pulled her over the back of the couch and across his lap. He grinned in triumph at his accomplished feat before his lips traveled up past her wrist to skim across her inner arm and the crook of her elbow.

"Your headache," she reminded him uncertainly.

"Has been replaced by a much stronger ache elsewhere," he informed her, his voice husky with desire.

"I guess I'll have to soothe that too," she murmured, her free hand loosening his tie completely and letting it slip to the floor.

"You're the only one who can," he confessed before his mouth sought hers in an intoxicating caress that aroused a surge of excitement throughout her body. Karyn proceeded to demonstrate her opinion of him as a man, her

165

tempting actions driving all other thoughts right out of his mind.

"This time, let's go upstairs to bed," she suggested boldly, letting her lips wander over his strong jawline.

Christopher readily agreed and in one fluid movement pulled her into an upright position and stood close behind her, lovingly molding her to him. She could feel the powerful tension in the lean body behind her when he bent down to whisper intimate promises, his voice warm and soft against her ear as he evocatively told her exactly what he intended to do. His lips brushed across her lobe and caressed the sensitive skin behind her ear, his lightly flickering tongue sending tremors up and down her body that left her quivering in expectation.

His hand slid down to softly stroke her collarbone before using it to press her tightly against him and propel her up the stairs to their room. Once there, his hands spanned her waist as he turned her around and gathered her close, her body neatly fitting in the curve of his. Deep blue eyes glowed down at her with unconcealed hunger.

"I need you so much," Christopher muttered, his voice oddly shaken. "I don't know how I ever managed without you. I love you, and I want you—God, how I want you," he groaned.

His lips took hers, her warm and pliant mouth returning his kiss. Tasting her honeyed response, his vagrant lips, wandered and enticed, beguilingly stroking hers until they clung helplessly to his. His hand slipped through her hair to the nape of her neck, while his soft seductive voice muttered disjointed endearments in between kisses.

Karyn thrust her fingers into his thick hair and felt the pounding thunder of his heart against her breasts where they were crushed against him. Somehow his shirt was undone and discarded; her fingers were then free to run up and down the broad expanse of his chest, rubbing the muscular skin. She felt his body shudder and he groaned her name before gathering her closer. His hands were now roaming restlessly under her camisole top, their movement on her skin almost an act of love in itself. When the thin top drifted to the floor, his trailing fingers faithfully followed the line of her body from her smooth shoulders down across the side of her breast, the inward curve of her waist, and the swell of her hips to her silky thighs. Her cotton shorts soon joined the top on the floor and she stood shivering in front of him. The room still retained the heat from earlier in the day, so her tremors weren't caused by any chill, but rather by his languorous appraisal and the raw desire reflected in the molten depths of his eyes as they raked her from head to toe.

Christopher quickly stripped and together they lay on the bed, his lips brushing over her eyelids and long lashes, before covering her face with kisses. Her body was urgently aware of his when she burrowed closer. She sensed in him a desperate need to display his prowess as a lover capable of satisfying a woman. Before she lost herself in the flow of feeling, she determined that she would bring him with her to the heights he was taking her to. And so she reciprocated his passion and control measure for measure, hands stroking at will, lips caressing with each touch.

"What are you doing?" he breathed indistinctly against her warm skin.

"The same thing you're doing to me," Karyn answered unsteadily. "Should I stop?"

"God no," he muttered, his voice taut with unrestrained desire, and he encouraged her on to further impassioned experimentation.

Feeling his rapidly increasing arousal, her body arched against his. At that moment her very existence seemed dependent on his touch. Their ardor was inflamed to a volcanic pitch of racing heartbeats, uneven breathing, and intimately entwined limbs. At the culmination of their passion Karyn gave a breathless cry of joy as her system

167

exploded in a fiery display of propulsive sensations. She felt his convulsive answering movements and groans of gratification as they were transported to the realm of the senses. In both giving totally of themselves, they received their reward tenfold, reaching a higher plateau of pleasure than ever before because of the careful construction of its groundwork.

Her limbs felt as soft as butter when she lay in his arms afterwards, her leg casually thrown across his, her head resting on his shoulder. Her heart was filled with a drowsy sweetness as she listened to his heart beating against her cheek. She snuggled closer, feeling at home in his arms, secure at last. His hand rested on the softness of her body, stroking her here and there, while her fingers walked up his chest to caress the outline of his warm lips and smooth across the rough texture of his cheeks. Both of them were fully indulging in the freedom and enjoyment of touching one another.

Lifting her face to his, Christopher appreciated the slanting, luminous green eyes, the flushed curve of her cheek, the small tilted nose, and the fullness of her trembling lips that had so recently caressed his. This was his wife, the woman he loved more than anything else in the world. He tenderly lowered his head to gently kiss her, glad that she was now protected from Stella's viciousness. But he had an uneasy feeling that something or someone else might still threaten their happiness.

Karyn vaguely heard the alarm go off the next morning and protested sleepily when she felt her husband leave her side to lean over and turn it off. She felt him sit up in bed and reluctantly stretched her limbs, catlike, before sitting up behind him to rest her chin upon his bare shoulder.

"Do you have to go?" she tempted languidly.

"Unfortunately, yes," he groaned, turning his head to admire the picture she made, sitting in the middle of the tumbled bed, her body only loosely covered by his pajama top, the shadowy cleft between the curve of her pale breasts clearly visible by the deep V of the neckline. The cloud of her titian hair was in a glorious disarray around her shining face, the drowsy depths of her emerald eyes still savoring the memory of last night's passion.

"I have to drive to Tinley Park for a meeting with a client this morning, but I'll come home early," Christopher promised. Catching her straying fingers and lifting them to his mouth, he playfully went on to nip them.

"I wouldn't if I were you," she cautioned.

"No?"

Karyn shook her head. "You're in a much more vulnerable position than I am," proving it by running the ridge of her white teeth across his exposed shoulder. She was surprised and excited to see goose bumps appear along the length of his arm due to her actions.

"Now I know where you're vulnerable," she teased.

"I'm vulnerable all over where you're concerned," Christopher returned, the deep timbre of his voice pleasantly affecting her senses. "Now stop trying to lead me astray," he instructed.

"Me? I didn't do anything," she protested.

"Not yet, but you'd like to and so would I," he said dryly. "The sooner I go, the sooner I'll be back. I want to take my time and enjoy you."

Karyn reluctantly let him go, pulling on a silk robe and belting it around her trim waist before following him to the bathroom, where he began shaving.

"What would you like for breakfast?" she stood in the bathroom doorway to ask.

"You!" he growled, making a grab for her.

"Uh, uh," she mockingly chastised him from across the room, where she'd safely fled. "You had your chance!"

Noting the late hour, she decided that breakfast would have to be a hurried affair because of the time they'd already wasted on this morning. Wasted—she thought to herself in amazement—no way! She'd much rather have spent the time as they had, satisfying other appetites. You could eat with anyone, but love shared with one special man was something else again!

The water for his morning coffee was put on to boil, then a package of French crumb cupcakes were pulled out of the freezer and put in the microwave. Pushing the space-age technology sensor buttons, she felt a twinge of insecurity. Karyn hadn't really gotten accustomed to using the microwave yet, confused by the profusion of power levels and temperature probes. Christopher laughed at her apprehensive expression when he walked into the kitchen.

"Anyone would think you were programming a multifunctioning computer instead of a simple microwave," he ridiculed her.

"Never insult the cook," she retorted haughtily. "It tends to be dangerous. One never knows what one might find in one's food."

His blue eyes laughed at her. "Does that mean I'll find a miniature blond jumping out of one of these cupcakes?" he asked hopefully.

The breakfast was quickly downed, and grabbing his briefcase from the chair near the front door, Christopher turned to pull her into a close embrace. Their lips merged with a heady magnetism that colored her heart with exhilarating joy. Her fingers kneaded the muscles along his wide shoulders before moving along the strong nape of his neck.

"I don't know how I'm going to keep my mind on business this morning," he muttered, nudging the hollows under her ear with his nose and enjoying the clean, sweet scent of her, while his lips ran over the delicate skin of her throat. He drew a shaky breath as he pulled away, shaking his head regretfully at the slow smile of invitation on her face. A lean masculine finger smoothed the drifting strands of her coppery cloud of hair away from her beguiling features. Drawing her distracting hands down from his shoulders, he placed a tender kiss in the center of each palm, then closed her hand around it.

"Hold on to that until I get back," he gruffly instructed her before turning to walk out the door.

CHAPTER ELEVEN

Christopher was pleased that his morning conference with Mr. Rayland and the executives of Rayland Manufacturing had gone well. This last meeting practically wrapped up their month-long negotiations to evaluate and replace the company's entire programming system, a choice assignment and a major accomplishment for a growing firm like Christopher's. Unlocking the door to his car, he noticed a leaden heaviness in the sultry, humid air. The past few days had been unseasonably hot for so early in the summer. Although it was only a little after noon, the sky had begun to darken along the western horizon. The air was still, but the cumulous clouds seemed to roll by quickly, like churning gray waves in an alarming sea.

Pulling out of the parking lot, Christopher turned the car's air-conditioning system on. The blowers cooled the hot, stagnant air inside, but drowned out the rumbling thunder of the approaching storm. His thoughts were so filled with last night's deeply moving experience and this afternoon's anticipated continuance that he didn't notice the increasing murkiness of the sky or the expectant hush that fell over everything—the proverbial calm before the storm.

When the rain came, it was as if the heavens had suddenly split open. It came down in torrents, deluging the streets and making travel extremely difficult. The car's windshield wipers were on high, but they were a frail protection against the blinding curtain of water that covered the front window. His headlights were turned on as the seething darkness that had been on the horizon such a short time ago arrived with a vengeance. His smothered curse accompanied the ominous echoing clatter of hailstones bouncing off the roof and hood of his car. The boiling sky had taken on a forboding, sickly pea-green cast. As abruptly as it had begun, the lashing precipitation ceased. The deadly stillness was suddenly broken by the rising wind, buffeting the helpless victims in its path.

Christopher's firm long fingers tightly gripped the steering wheel, struggling to keep the car from being blown off the road. There was no place to stop, no safe shelter from the turbulent cauldron of the storm. Evergreens and willows were nearly bent over, while more inflexible trees had their branches ripped off as they tried to stand firm in the face of the howling wind.

There was no warning of what was to come. With an alarming crack, one of the trees suddenly gave up the fight, striking his car as it crashed to the ground. Christopher's inert form slumped over the steering wheel.

Karyn had just finished cleaning the kitchen when she heard the thunder growling in the distance. Looking outside the window, she could see that a thunderstorm was approaching. She raced upstairs to shut most of the windows, then returned back downstairs to call the weather information number. As she'd suspected from the hot, muggy weather all morning, there was a tornado watch in effect until late afternoon due to an approaching cool front that would relieve the heat, but only after some often violent storms.

Coming from Nebraska, in the center of the tornado belt of the midwestern United States, Karyn knew what to do to be prepared. She left the windows on the southwestern side of the house open a bit to relieve the built-up pressure that could cause the house to explode in the path of a tornado. The radio was kept on for additional weather bulletins, and Mouse was locked in the downstairs bathroom for safety. Although the sky was getting darker, it lacked the garish inky-green glow that usually accompanied dangerous storms. Several inches of rain were dumped before the system moved on. Good thing I didn't water the garden this morning, she thought to herself with a smile.

She opened the back door after the storm passed and was relieved to find that the air was slightly cooler and not as humid as before. The cool front appeared to have arrived. She hoped the storm hadn't tied Christopher up in traffic; he was already late. Reaching into the refrigerator to pour herself a cool glass of lemonade, she froze when she heard the words Tinley Park in the news broadcast on the radio. She raced over to listen closely.

'While no offical sightings of funnel clouds were reported by the police, a destructive storm did hit Tinley Park at about 12:20 this afternoon. A number of trees are down; power and phone lines are out in many areas; and widespread damage is reported. Several roofs were blown off and a nearby trailer park had half a dozen trailers overturned. We don't have any information on how many people have been injured. Police and emergency vehicles are in the area now. We'll give you more information as it becomes available. On the stock market today . . .'

Karyn turned the sound back down with trembling fingers. Christopher had said his meeting this morning was in Tinley Park, and he was already late coming home. She racked her brains trying to recall if he had given her the name of the firm. It took her horror-stricken mind several minutes to think of calling his office downtown for the name of the company. She could've screamed in frustration when she had to dial the number twice, her fingers hitting the wrong push-button numbers on the phone in her haste to get through.

"This is Mrs. Reid, Christopher's wife. I believe he had an appointment in Tinley Park this morning; could you please give me the company's name, and phone number, if you have that as well?"

"Certainly, just a minute please . . . ." She heard the click as she was put on hold. It seemed like an age, but it was only a few seconds later when the voice came back with the information.

"Mr. Reid had a meeting scheduled for 10:30 this morning with Mr. Rayland at Rayland Manufacturing in Tinley Park. I'm afraid I don't have their number right here, but if you'd like to hold, I can check around and see if anyone knows."

"No, that's all right, I'll find it myself," Karyn told them. "Thank you."

She hung up before they could answer, deciding to forgo the phone directory and call information. It rang fourteen times before someone answered. Karyn was suffering from anxiety-caused distortion: seconds became minutes and minutes became hours. Once she obtained the number, she had to try it several times because the line was busy. She was ready to burst into tears when she finally got through and asked for Mr. Rayland.

"Mr. Rayland's office, can I help you?"

"I'd like to speak to Mr. Rayland, please."

"May I ask who's calling?"

"Mrs. Reid."

"One moment, please." On hold again.

"John Rayland, speaking."

"Mr. Rayland, this is Mrs. Christopher Reid. I believe you had an appointment with my husband this morning. Can you tell me, is he still there?" she asked hopefully.

"No, he left at lunchtime; said he had another very important appointment for this afternoon."

"I'm sorry, Mr. Rayland, but could you be a little more specific. Did he leave before or after the storm?"

"That was some storm, wasn't it?" he exclaimed. "Christopher left right before it hit. Luckily we didn't have any damage, although I did hear that it was a close call. Apparently there was a lot of damage just a few blocks from here, and I hear that Route 19 is closed because of flooding and downed trees."

"Thank you, Mr. Rayland," Karyn said shakily.

"Not at all. I'm sorry I couldn't be of more help."

Maybe his car had gotten stalled—a logical assumption with all the flooding from the downpour. Or the traffic could have been backed up due to detours around the affected area. These were all possibilities and one of them was probably what was keeping Christopher, she tried to reassure herself.

Within an hour that reassurance had disappeared. It was nearly five, and if anything minor had made him late, he would have been home by now. Karyn was desperate, terrified by a dreadful premonition that something ghastly had happened to her husband. Perhaps the panic was even greater coming after the exultation they had shared the night before. It was as though the pendulum of her emotions had swung full circle: experiencing the heights last night, she was now plumbing the depths of fear.

Her thoughts were such a chaotic jumble that she couldn't concentrate on what her next course of action would be. Dismay rolled over her in voiceless waves. Some other part of herself took over, automatically dialing the Tinley Park hospital. The emergency room informed her that they were still receiving the injured and therefore couldn't say whether or not Christopher Reid was a patient. They suggested calling back later, after six.

Their noninformative reply gave her a strong feeling of déjà vu. For a moment she was transported back in time to that infamous night in Chicago when she'd frantically tried to locate her new husband.

When the phone rang, she jumped, grabbing it off the wall before it had even completed one ring.

"Hello?" she quickly answered.

"Karyn, it's Marie. I thought I'd check to see how you're doing with the storms and all. You do know there's a tornado watch out, don't you?"

"Yes, Marie, I know." Disappointment was evident in her strained voice.

"What's wrong? You don't sound very good. Has something happened?"

"Christopher was supposed to be home several hours ago. He was up in Tinley Park, and I heard on the radio that they were hit with a severe storm that caused a lot of damage. Oh, Marie," she choked, "I'm so afraid something awful has happened."

"Calm down. Maybe he's been delayed by all the flooding. I just heard on the local news that a lot of the streets in that area are blocked off and traffic is being rerouted. Unfortunately, Jerry has a meeting tonight or I'd leave the kids with him and come over to keep you company."

"That's all right. Thank you for thinking of it."

"Listen, if you need any help, call me. I'll be home all night. I'll hang up now so that if Christopher is trying to call, he won't get a busy signal."

"Thanks, Marie."

"Not at all. Don't forget to call if you need anything, anything at all. Good-bye."

"Bye."

As the minutes ticked by, her nervous system clinically registered the alarming signals of her distress. Tears rained down her cheeks. Her hands trembled and grew cold as ice. She walked back and forth across the floor in a tumult of despair and anguish. A series of plaintive meows reminded her that Mouse was still locked in the bathroom. Once freed, the kitten sensed her mistress's distraught state and stayed close by.

The rush of panic was impossible to contain, and it eventually overwhelmed her with its blanket of inexpressible dread. She sat on the edge of an uncomfortable straight chair, which was placed in front of the picture window facing the driveway. Filled with fear, she crawled into a cave of despair, curling herself up and rocking back and forth. Incoherent prayers trembled from her lips and mixed with the saltiness of her tears. Her mind had stopped functioning; she felt frozen inside. The only thing she was capable of doing was staring out the window, willing Christopher to appear.

The pit of her stomach dropped alarmingly when she saw a police car pull up in front of the house. She closed her eyes, cringing in horror, her heart pounding in her ears. He's dead, she tortured herself. The police have come to ask me to identify the body. Oh my God, he's dead! Her hands bruised her body as they gripped it in a convulsion of agony.

She heard the doorbell ring but was incapable of answering it. She was paralyzed with terror. The door was pushed open, and she looked up to see the outlines of two bodies silhouetted against the door frame. Her entire body shook with emotion, until she heard a beloved voice uncertainly call out, "Karyn?"

He was alive! Leaping to her feet, she reached Christopher just as he flicked on the light switch. The illumination showed them face to face, her pale, distraught features hungrily staring at his ashen face, his eyes darkened with pain and reflecting some kind of shock. She noted the white bandage over his right eyebrow, and the police officer offering his arm in support, while Christopher stood there swaying with exhaustion.

"I'm Officer Atken, Mrs. Reid. Your husband had a slight run-in with a tree during this afternoon's storm. His wound was stitched up at the hospital. Nothing serious."

"Christopher," she finally croaked, reaching out with

eager, loving hands to gently guide him to the couch in the living room. Karyn collected her scattered wits enough to thank the officer before he left. When she sat down next to Christopher her composure crumbled and the tears coursed down her face, while her hands explored his arms and shoulders to confirm that he was indeed alive and here beside her.

"Are you all right?" she kept repeating through it all. His hands came up to tenderly wipe the tears from her face, but as soon as he did, they were replaced by more.

"I'm okay," he answered gruffly.

She plied him with questions, interspersed with soft kisses. "Why didn't you call? Where's the car? What happened?"

"The phone lines were out, so I couldn't call. A tree was blown down by the fierce wind, and the damned thing smashed the hood of my car, cracking the engine block. They towed it away—I'm not sure if it was totaled or not. But Karyn, something else was smashed as well," he continued urgently. "The wall blocking my memory."

She pulled away to stare up at him, her damp green eyes wide in amazement.

"It's true," he firmly answered the unspoken question on her face. "I know what happened, and why I left you on our honeymoon night!"

CHAPTER TWELVE

Karyn sat in silence, her hand clasping his as the bizarre story unfolded before her. Two years before, Christopher had flown into Chicago's O'Hare International Airport from London, on his way to Nebraska. The international flight's departure from London had been delayed, so he missed his connecting flight and had to spend a good deal of the night in the airport.

At around three in the morning he'd been awakened by a commotion near the airline freight office and had glimpsed the face of a man fleeing past him with a bag in his hands. This man was followed shortly thereafter by several armed guards. The police were called in, and Christopher was held for questioning as the only witness to a robbery of several million dollars worth of diamonds. A police artist drew up a sketch of the man Christopher had seen, and a warrant was put out for his arrest. Apparently, he was involved with the Mafia and had been suspected in other similar cases, but the police had never been able to prove anything.

Christopher was allowed to continue on to Lincoln with instructions to check in with a Lieutenant Clark if he would be moving or changing status. He was also instructed not to talk to anyone about the case. Christopher followed both instructions and periodically kept in touch with the lieutenant. The case was going well. The suspect, Sam Kemp, had been apprehended and was being kept in jail without bond on the basis of Christopher's identification. The law enforcement agency was looking forward to the trial, pleased that this criminal would finally be put behind bars. However, the officials also knew that Kemp was but a small link in the hierarchy of the mafiosi. They suspected that one of the local syndicate leaders, Leo Gambucci, was responsible for the planning of the heist and were hoping that the robber would plea bargain and turn state's evidence against this leading crime figure.

And so it was that Christopher had phoned Lieutenant Clark with the information that he was getting married and would be stopping in Chicago for one night before continuing on for a two-month honeymoon in England. The trial wasn't scheduled until his return, so there would be no conflict there. In fact, the lieutenant was pleased that Christopher would be out of the country for a while because he had heard disturbing rumors on the street lately and was getting worried about Christopher's safety. But the lieutenant himself was working undercover, trying to provide the link between the robber and the gangleader, so he wasn't able to spend much time with that concern.

At about eight o'clock on the first evening of their honeymoon, Christopher had gotten an urgent call from the lieutenant, who told him that he had to meet him and gave Christopher the address. The lieutenant said that it was a matter of life and death and that it was to be kept in the strictest confidence.

Christopher left the hotel and met the lieutenant as arranged. He was shocked to find him badly beaten, barely able to gasp out that there was a contract out on Christopher's life and that he was to leave town immediately. The police would be able to assist him in that respect, but he had to leave without delay and take his wife with him. The mob knew that he had gotten married and were not above using Karyn as a means of getting to Christopher.

After imparting this information, the lieutenant had

died in Christopher's arms. Events passed quickly after that. Twin beams of a car's headlights were aimed directly at him. Christopher ran and the car followed, gaining on him every second. It was only a matter of time before he was struck from behind.

He lay on the pavement, barely conscious, as someone got out of the car and rifled through his pockets, pulling out his wallet. Then they grabbed his hand and yanked off his wedding ring. When he tried to protest, a voice above him snarled, "You ain't gonna need this where you're goin', buddy. This'll prove to the big man that we finished the job. Just close your eyes, and you won't feel a thing."

Raised voices and running feet impinged on the fringe of Christopher's consciousness. Someone was coming. His attacker panicked and took off, the car tires squealing as he fled down the street.

I have to hide Karyn, Christopher thought; I can't let them find her. Have to hide her. Then all thought was covered by the dark cloud of unconsciousness that overcame him.

The group of people that found him called an ambulance, and he was taken to the nearest hospital trauma center, which was in a neighboring suburb. His accident had taken place just outside the city limits of Chicago.

"That's the whole story," he concluded.

So this was why he'd forgotten her. In trying to protect her from harm he'd hidden her so effectively that he couldn't find her himself! The puzzle fell into place, and Karyn realized that her heart had been correct—Christopher had never stopped loving her. In fact, the only thing strong enough to block out the memory of her had been the dire need to protect her.

"What happened to the case? Why didn't the police try to locate you after the accident? I mean, you have been walking around Chicago for the past year under your correct name of Christopher Reid. The syndicate wouldn't have had that much trouble locating you. You've been in constant danger all this time!" she exclaimed in horror as realization dawned. "I think you should call the police right away. Who was the captain who was in charge?"

"Captain Wieth."

Karyn got up and carried the telephone over to the couch. "Here, call him." Her voice was strained with fear.

Christopher did so only to find that Captain Wieth had retired right after Christopher's accident. "You should speak to Captain Linkowski—he took over that position. But he won't be in until nine in the morning, so I suggest you call back then."

"Thank you," and he hung up.

"That was fast, what did they say?"

He explained the situation to her. "I guess there's nothing we can do until tomorrow then," she conceded.

"I also remember about Stella," he announced.

Karyn was aghast. "Was she their moll or something?" she asked in a horrified voice.

"No," he weakly laughed. "She was my uncle's nurse. I met her a few times when I came to visit him. I now know that I never lived in Milwaukee, and she knew it, too. The lie served the purpose of relocating me so you couldn't find me. My uncle had written me in one of his last letters, saying that he'd fired her for unprofessional behavior. She knew that I was the only relative and would therefore stand to inherit the firm, and she wanted a piece of the action." Christopher leaned his head back against the couch, exhausted by the revelation of the truth.

"God," he muttered in disgust, "I hope I never see that woman again, or I won't be responsible for my actions. When I think of all the time she wasted for us, and the torture she put us through, I could . . ."

"Darling," Karyn intervened softly, "I think she's been punished enough already."

He looked at her in surprise. "In what way?" he demanded.

"She lost you, and that's a terrible punishment to take. Now how about some warm broth and then bed."

She went into the kitchen to prepare it for him and returned shortly with some beef broth and soda crackers. She watched over him like a hawk until he ate every last bit.

"Are you dizzy? Do you think you can make it up the stairs if I help you?"

"With you helping me I can do anything," he teased her unsteadily.

She smiled as she helped him up, but it only temporarily hid the concern she felt for him. His pallor was alarming, and he leaned heavily on her while they made their way upstairs. She soon got him safely in bed and joined him, careful not to bounce the bed when she got in.

He began muttering restlessly in the middle of the night. Her hand reached out to feel his forehead, but it was cool. She lovingly smoothed back his tousled hair, careful not to disturb the bandages covering the wound on his forehead. He turned to her, sensing even in his sleep that here was a source of tender comfort. Unheard reassurances were whispered to him, their soothing tone and her soft touch communicating her everlasting love and acting as a tranquilizing panacea for his suffering.

His head was pillowed against the concave curve of her shoulder. The uniform evenness of his breathing feathered across the hollow between her breasts, giving rise to an almost maternal desire to shield him from harm.

Christopher shifted slightly against her cushioning softness before he fell into a peaceful slumber. Karyn lay there for some time monitoring him, not falling asleep herself until she was certain that he was truly at ease, reflecting on their love and praying that the danger hanging over them would soon be dispelled.

His movement awakened her the next morning. "I had the strangest dream last night," he lazily murmured. "I was visited by an angel."

She gazed down into his sleepy blue eyes with some misgiving, fearful that he might be light-headed. Her face must have reflected those thoughts because he assured her, "I'm not hallucinating, although seeing a beautiful vision such as yourself first thing in the morning could easily be mistaken for that! Other than a thumping headache, I feel perfectly alright," and, as if to demonstrate the fact, he went to get out of bed.

"Where do you think you're going?" she demanded fiercely.

"Just to the washroom. Do I have your permission?" he mocked her.

"Oh," she blushed. "Well, so long as you come right back to bed."

Christopher sent her a deliciously lustful leer and answered, "How could I refuse an invitation like that? You bet I'll be right back!"

A few minutes later he did indeed return, but his features were drawn with the effort. She hurriedly got up and helped him into bed, their earlier flirtation forgotten.

"Do you want me to call the doctor?"

"No, it's just a bang on the head."

"Then the least you can do is stay in bed today and take it easy. I'll go get you some breakfast so you can take one of those painkillers you brought home with you from the hospital."

He subsided back against the pillows and obeyed her orders, proof that he was not up to par. She brought him a light breakfast of soft-boiled egg and toast with some weak tea. He had just swallowed his pill when he asked, "What time is it?"

"It's a little after nine."

"Give me the phone, will you? I'll call Captain Linkowski about the case."

Karyn dialed the number for him, and the captain answered his extension.

"Linkowski here."

"Captain Linkowski, my name is Christopher Reid. I believe you've taken over the position that Captain Wieth had?"

"That's correct."

"Captain Wieth was working on a case that involved me in May of last year. It was a robbery of several million dollars worth of diamonds from the airport."

"Mr. Reid, would you hold on a minute? I think I know the case you're referring to, but I want to pull the files on it. I wasn't involved myself, so I'm not familiar with it. Just a minute."

He soon returned. "Mr. Reid, I now see why you're calling. First off, let me assure you that you are perfectly safe. The department was remiss in not notifying you of this sooner, and I apologize, but Captain Wieth was suffering from ill health at the time the case was closed. He has since retired."

"I don't understand." Christopher's voice reflected his confusion. "What happened?"

"The man you were going to testify against is dead, as is the man who instigated the contract to kill you. They were both murdered by a syndicate rival."

"But I thought Kemp was in jail?"

"He was granted bail and set free. Of course, he was only the hired help. We suspected that the planning was done by reputed mobster Leo Gambucci. He's the one who put out the contract on you. The moment Kemp was freed, he headed straight for Gambucci's mansion where they were both killed. So you see why I said that you are no longer in any danger."

"What about the diamonds?" Christopher asked. "Were they ever recovered?"

"Yes, they were. Believe it or not, they were found on airport ground, stuffed in a locker at the other end of the terminal."

"So it's all over?"

"Yes, it is. I'd like to apologize again for any anxiety the department's oversight has caused. We want you to know that your valiant behavior was appreciated."

"Thank you, Captain."

"Not at all. I hope that settles any remaining questions you had. If you should think of anything else, please feel free to call me."

Karyn was still completely in the dark, having only heard Christopher's end of the conversation. She grabbed his arm the moment he hung up the phone. "What did he say?"

"You don't have to worry anymore. The case is closed." He went on to relay what Captain Linkowski had told him.

Karyn sent up a fervent prayer of thankfulness, tears of relief rolling down her cheeks.

"I hope these are the last tears you'll ever have to cry on my account," he solemnly declared.

They spent a quiet day, Christopher sleeping off the aftereffects of the painkiller he'd taken earlier. He insisted on getting dressed and going downstairs for dinner. Karyn's protests went unheard; however, she was allowed to assist him in getting dressed. Her unsteady fingers carefully buttoned up his shirt.

His slight chuckle made her look up and ask, "Did I tickle you?"

He shook his head very slowly, due to the pain caused otherwise. "You skipped a button," pointing to the uneven hem at the bottom.

"I haven't had much experience dressing men," she spiritedly defended herself.

"Have you had much experience undressing them, then?" he teased with a devilish glint in his sparkling blue eyes.

"No, but I learn quickly."

"I know you do!" he agreed with intimate appreciation.

Later that night in their bedroom Karyn heard the bathroom door shut in the darkness. A shadowy figure silently padded its way across the room to the bed.

"Who is it?" she whispered, knowing what the answer would be.

"It's your husband," Christopher whispered back. "Remember me?"

"Remind me," she invited.

He did so with a thoroughness that rendered her breathless. His warm hands glided across the slippery material of her negligee, brailling her in the darkness until he found the veiled riches he was urgently seeking and manipulated them to pulsating life.

"Ummm," she purred, her voice heavy with appreciation and anticipation. "That feels familiar. Jog my memory a little more."

His lips coaxed hers apart, relishing their sweetness before capturing them completely, stifling her dazzled gasp of ecstasy as he jogged her memory a *lot* more!

Morning's pale light was filtering through a crack in the curtains when the solid form Karyn was resting against moved, in spite of her protests. Her drowsy green eyes opened to rest on the muscular ridges of her husband's back. He was preparing to get up when her soft voice stopped him. "I hope you weren't thinking of going to work today."

"Actually, I was contemplating doing more than just thinking about it," he replied.

"Well, forget it," she declared emphatically.

"Please, no jokes about my amnesia this early in the morning."

"I'm not joking." Karyn pointed to the telephone on the end table. "Call your office, and tell them your wife won't let you out of bed."

"Do you think I'm up to it?" His expression was deliberately suggestive.

"What you can't handle, I will!" she informed him with an audacious look.

"Brazen hussy!" He leaned over to accompany his accusation with a kiss.

"That's me," she grinned cheerfully.

"You're certainly feeling your oats this morning."

"Not oats, darling. You!" She smiled at his smothered groan.

"Maybe I should lie back and let you have your wicked way with me," he murmured huskily. "But on the other hand," which he placed in a very intimate spot, "this body is too good to pass up."

"I was hoping you'd say that."

"And do this?"

Her breath caught in her throat at his tantalizing maneuvers. The warmth and power of the lean body pressed against hers was awesome. She returned his caresses with eager abandonment, her questing fingers gliding over him. Moving in unison, the timeless alchemy of sensual perceptions took over. The outside world slipped away as they were caught up in the pulsating pleasures of love.

"THE MOST ROMANTIC NOVEL SINCE LOVE STORY."
—Good Housekeeping

Change of Heart

SALLY MANDEL

Once in a long while, a story is so bursting with tenderness that its charm is irresistible.

That story is Sharlie and Brian's story, *Change of Heart*— a love story for a lifetime.

A Dell Book $2.95 (11355-5)